MR ALFRED M.A.

George Friel (1910–75), was born and brought up in a two room flat in Maryhill Road in Glasgow, the city where he was to work for the rest of his career. Educated at St Mungo's Academy, he was the only one in a family of seven children to go to university where he took an Ordinary MA, before training as a teacher at Jordanhill College. He married his wife Isabel in 1938 and the couple moved to Bishopbriggs where they were to stay for the rest of their lives. When war broke out Friel served in the RAOC before returning to teaching, a profession he gradually came to hate and distrust, although he never lost his concern for children. Such experience became the basis for *Mr Alfred MA*, and Friel's sense of autobiographical irony allowed him to share the title of his unpublished collection of poems with his hero. He became assistant head of a primary school before retiring in the early seventies.

Friel's first novel was *The Bank of Time* (1959). In all his books he determined to write about the mundane lives of ordinary people from his own working class background. His rather dark sense of humour and a rigorously intellectual style did not make him a popular author, although *The Boy Who Wanted Peace* (1964) sold well after its appearance on television. *Grace and Miss Partridge* (1969) was followed by *Mr Alfred MA* (1972), perhaps his most powerful novel. *An Empty House* appeared after the author's death from cancer in 1975.

George Friel

MR ALFRED M.A.

A NOVEL

Introduced by Douglas Gifford

CANONGATE
CLASSICS
8

First published in 1972 by Calder and Boyers Ltd.
First published as a Canongate Classic in 1987
by Canongate Publishing Limited
17 Jeffrey Street
Edinburgh EHI IDR

British Library Cataloguing in Publication Data
Friel, George
Mr Alfred M.A.—(Canongate classics).
I. Title
823'.914 [F]   PR6056.R53

ISBN 0–86241–163–7

The publishers gratefully acknowledge
general subsidy from the Scottish Arts Council
towards the Canongate Classics series
and a specific grant towards the
publication of this title

Set in 10pt Plantin
by Alan Sutton Publishing Ltd, Gloucester
Printed and bound in Great Britain
by Cox and Wyman Ltd, Reading

Introduction

This is one of the greatest of Scottish novels. It is a passionate denunciation of what is happening in Glasgow's neglected peripheral housing schemes, and a statement which uncomfortably jolts fashionable new complacency about Glasgow's revival and rediscovery of a 'dear green place' identity. It is a novel which anticipated the 'new wave' realism, vitality, and scepticism of Glasgow writers like Tom Leonard, James Kelman, and Alasdair Gray — indeed, only *Mr Alfred MA* can stand alongside Kelman's *A Chancer* (1985) and Gray's *Lanark* (1981) for intellectual power, controlled concern, and artistic achievement. And like them, it is in the end not to be read simply within a Scottish cultural context, but as a major European statement about the breakdown of traditional values, of community, and most important of all, breakdown of communication.

When Auberon Waugh reviewed this novel in *The Spectator* in 1972, he complained of Friel's 'extraordinary notion of fine writing'. This consisted, said Waugh, of Friel collecting obscure words from places like *The British Pharmacopœia* and throwing them together with 'equally unfamiliar slang expressions from Clydeside'. Waugh quoted from Friel's description of the quarrel of Gerard Provan with his sister Senga.

> The anapaests of his bawling were hammered out by his punches . . . poised to jouk, right hand over right ear, left hand over left ear, her head sinistral, she borde the kitchensink, in defence of temporary kyphosis.

It's true that most readers won't know many of the words here (although 'jouk' hardly deserves Waugh's English condescension). But in missing entirely Friel's ironic comment on breakdown of communication between novel and reader, due to the proliferation of modern jargons and increasing illiteracy, Waugh missed the entire point of the novel. Friel was arguing that communication through language and gesture was disintegrating in a society in which family ties, validity of education, and the sense of self and identity gained from these, were disintegrating also.

Friel had been developing this theme in previous novels, outstandingly *The Boy Who Wanted Peace* (1964) and *Grace and Miss Partridge* (1969). Both present protagonists who are failed idealists (much like those of the novels of Robin Jenkins), and both place them in a materialistic and decaying society — decaying both physically, in terms of buildings and amenities, and spiritually. Friel valued the family unit above all other social institutions, but where the earlier novels had shown some hope of regeneration in their mixture of satire and humane comedy, it seems to me that Friel's vision darkens in *Mr Alfred*, to the point where he wonders if any valid communication between the different parts of society is possible. No easy analysis is offered; ambivalence is ubiquitous (a recurrent feature of Scottish fiction); and central to this ambivalence is the figure of Mr Alfred himself.

No one who knows Joyce's *Portrait of the Artist as a Young Man* can fail to see Friel's debt to his master. It's not just a matter of wordplay and serious punning, or the desire to do for Glasgow reality what *Dubliners* did for that city: there is a deeper closeness, in the enigmatic view each author takes of his protagonist. Stephen Dedalus may be sensitive, the embryonic artist; he may also be pretentious and selfish towards his family and society. All his talk of higher duty may be evasion of an honest admission of insufficiency. It is also true of Mr Alfred. His love of the language of Shakespeare and Milton, his apparent appreciation of finer nuances in literature and life, his position in the novel as a kind of martyr to the growth of materialistic philistinism, may all be questioned. He is a failed poet; his student volume *Negotiations for a Treaty*, can symbolise either a noble attempt to bridge the two worlds of the Ideal and the Real, or his pathetic failure to negotiate a working compromise with life.

He's not necessarily a pathetic remnant of cultural value; he may also be the *cause* of much of the sickness in the world he loathes. He admits he hasn't in years read a book by a man younger than himself; he drinks to avoid reality; his 'affair' with Rose indicates his pathetic inability to make bridges with other human beings. Friel allows a reading here which sees this English teacher as representing (in exaggerated outline) the failure of English, as a subject, to communicate, connect, inspire imagination, deal with actuality, talk to its clientele.

Mr Alfred has little to offer to stimulate his aggressive young pupils. Instead, he retreats to his inoffensive younger girls' classes, just as around him his colleagues retreat to the safety of crosswords and pointless and interminable discussion of the rights and wrongs of belting children. Marvellously, Friel, the elusive but guiding author makes ironic comments throughout on the irrelevance of their activities; 'view an orphan hasn't got', the crossword clue, is of course 'panorama', filled in at the end of a staffroom debate which has never related to the human needs of its throughput, the children.

Friel controls the matter of Mr Alfred's 'affair' with Rose Weipers with delicacy and ironic detachment. Is the teacher sexually attracted, sexually guilty? Or is Rose the Glasgow version of a Joycean rose of imagination and idealism, innocent and sweet? We are never to know for sure – but we do know that this little girl, like Grace in *Grace and Miss Partridge*, is hardly the unsullied flower of her teacher's wistful dreams. She is a hoyden, and Friel makes a typically cruel juxtaposition of Mr Alfred's ideal yearnings and Rose's gutter-learned abilities to defend herself effectively and raucously. Senga, with her sensitivity and integrity, is the real flower of young womanhood; but communication is never allowed between her and Mr Alfred, even though she sympathises with him more than Rose does.

Communication breaks down between Rose and Senga too; at the end of the novel their anti-climactic inability to resume their earlier friendship comments on the transitory nature of all human promises of love. And even if it can be argued that elsewhere in the novel decent human beings like Granny Lyons, or Enrico Ianello, have existed — what of them? They have been presented as failures, refugees, victims of the rising anarchism of the young. And it is the Young who are the targets of Friel's bitterness, as much as those headmasters and newspaper journalists and psychologists whose unfitness and glib jargonising he satirises so effectively. Friel calls his gallivanting and murdering youngsters 'colts' and 'fillies', mockingly naming them as Edenic, natural animals, the more to emphasize their utter lack of the natural graces or instincts which these more beautiful animals possess. Gerald Provan is the archetype of this new world, with him and his 'friends' emerging as the modern version of Yeats's 'great beast' of the Second Coming slouching in its city streets, a beast of aimless Youth. Significantly, he comes from a broken family; significantly, he is presented as deteriorating in articulation and communication as the novel progresses.

The novel's fragmentary, apparently random presentation of classroom and staffroom cynicism alternating with gangfights, persecution of the old and weak, muggings, and the absence of anything but selfishness and desire for the momentary thrill, seems to suggest that Friel sees little hope for society in the behaviour of the modern young. Senga perhaps . . . but Friel's final comment on her is that like so many nicer people, she's socially unattractive and misunderstood. There is a love affair which contrasts with Mr Alfred's unhealthy obsession, neatly related to it in that it is Rose's sister Martha who loves Graeme, the university student whose failure leads them to a pact of suicide — but this is hardly an example of alternative hopeful youth, however. And the affair gains poignancy from the post-mortems held by the teachers who all point out how they knew that Graeme should have been an Arts student, and shouldn't have taken science subjects. Once again communication has broken down, insofar as either they haven't got through to him or they haven't tried hard enough to guide him. Education fails the most promising of the youngsters here, although in keeping with the overall ambivalence of the novel it is also suggested that Graeme is sadly flawed and selfish, as he manoeuvres towards his goal of sex with Martha.

The novel was to have been called *The Writing on the Wall*; the publication of another novel with that title precluded this. But the final section keeps this title and is truly magnificent. There is no finer Scottish writing than this mixture of realism and horrific surrealism. Friel has built up to this, as Mr Alfred slides down the professional ladder, and then from sanity to breakdown. The satire on language, and its methodology of ironic juxtapositioning of jargons and reality, reaches triumphant conclusion in the grotesque litanies of the psychologists Jubb and Knight, or the collections of newspaper horror stories Mr Alfred assembles towards the end; but especially in the wonderful evocation of Wasteland Glasgow within which Mr Alfred goes mad. — What a metaphor for breakdown of communication in our time is that phoneless box from which Mr Alfred was going to call the powers-that-be to tell them what was wrong! And the shadowy figure of the Tod — the fox, the Devil, the spirit of all the Gerard Provans plus the sense of an organising malign intelligence — takes a worthy place alongside those other great Scottish presentations of the Prince of Darkness by Hogg and Stevenson. But the final vision transcends Scottishness, and in its expression of bleak negativity, Friel's *Mr Alfred M.A.* stands comparison with Golding's *Lord of the Flies* and Conrad's *Heart of Darkness*.

DOUGLAS GIFFORD

PART ONE

ONE

She passed for a widow when she went to Tordoch. She flitted across the river thinking nobody there would know her husband had left her. He was a longdistance lorrydriver, always coming or going and never saying much the few hours he was at home. He went to Manchester one day with a load of castings and vanished, lost and gone for ever, as untraced and untraceable as those banal snows some folk keep asking about. Not that she bothered to ask. She was a working-woman with a good overtime in the biscuit factory. She could do without his wages. The manless planet of her life moved round her son Gerald. He was Gerry to his schoolmates, but never to her. She always gave him his name in full. She thought it sounded right out the top drawer that way. That was why she chose it, though neither she nor her husband had ever any Gerald among their kin. She loved her Gerald fiercely. She loved him a lot more than she loved his little sister Senga. He was a good boy to her, but too kind and gentle perhaps, too innocent. She had always to be protecting him from the malice of the world. But that's what she was there for. He was tall for his age, blond and grinning. The girl was skinny, gingerhaired, crosseyed, freckled and nervous. She had loved her father because he used to cuddle her at bedtime. But after the row she got for asking where he was when they flitted she was afraid to mention his name again.

About a year later, say the week before Christmas, when she was turned eleven and Gerald was fourteen, he was thumping her hard because she wouldn't fry sausages for him at teatime, even after he told her twice. The anapaests of his bawling were hammered out by his punches.

'Aye, you'll do what I say and jump up when I speak for you know I'm your boss and you've got to obey.'

Eight scapular blows.

She whimpered and crouched, but she still defied him, and her mother came home earlier than expected and caught her red-eyed in the act. Gerald was glad to have a witness of his sister's disobedience and complained it wasn't the first time.

Mrs Provan stared at Senga, frightening her.

'You'd start a fight in an empty house you would,' she said. 'You bad little besom.'

She advanced speaking.

'You know damn well it's your place to make a meal for Gerald when I'm not in. I'm fed up telling you.'

Senga retreated silently.

Poised to jouk, right hand over right ear, left hand over left ear, her head sinistral, she borded the kitchensink in a defence of temporary kyphosis.

Mrs Provan halted.

Senga straightened.

'It was me set the table and made the tea,' she replied with spirit, confounding her mother and her brother in one strabismic glare. 'If he wants any more he can make it himself.'

'It's not a boy's place to go using a fryingpan,' said Mrs Provan. 'That's a girl's job. Your job.'

'It's him starts fights,' said Senga. 'Not me. It's him. Always giving orders.'

Her guard was dropped.

Her mother swooped and slapped her twice across the face, left to right and then right to left.

Gerald grinned.

Senga wept.

'I wish my daddy was here.'

Gerald chanted.

'Ha-ha-ha! Look at her, see! She wants to sit on her daddy's knee!'

'She'll wait a long time for that,' said Mrs Provan.

She put her arm round Gerald, ratifying their secret treaty, and Gerald rubbed his hip against her thighs.

TWO

Mr Alfred sagged at the bar, sipped his whisky and quaffed his beer, smiled familiarly to the jokes exchanged across the counter, and lit his fifth cigarette in an hour. His hand wavered to put the flame to the fag and his lips wobbled to put the fag to the flame. The man at his elbow chatted to the barmaid. The barmaid chatted to the man at his elbow. Propinquity and alcohol made him anxious to be sociable. He waited for an opening to slip in a bright word. After all, he knew the man at his elbow and the man at his elbow knew him. They had seen each other often enough. But neither admitted knowing the other's name, though he must have heard it countless times from Stella, who knew them all.

It grieved Mr Alfred. Sometimes he thought he was making a mistake frequenting a common pub with common customers and a common barmaid when he had nothing in common with them. In every pub he went to he recognised anonymous faces. For besides being a bachelor and a schoolmaster, a Master of Arts and the author of a volume of unpublished poems, the only child of poor but Presbyterian parents and now a middleaged orphan, he was a veteran pubcrawler. But it was his weakness to stand always on the fringe of company, smiling into the middle distance, happy only with a glass in his hand. He had been a wallflower since puberty. He wanted to love his fellowmen. When he was young he even hoped to love women. Now every door seemed locked, and without a key he was afraid to knock.

Stella drew a pint. The beer was brisk. She brought the glass down slowly from the horizontal to the vertical. She was pleased with the creamy head on it, not too much, not too little. With pride she served her customer.

'There! How's that for a good top? See what I do for you!'

The man at Mr Alfred's elbow put a big hand round the pint-measure. He grinned.

'Nothing to what I could do for you.'

'Ho-ho,' said Stella. 'I'm sure.'

Her frolic smile said enough for a book on sex without fear. Mr Alfred caught a reprint tossed to him free. He jerked and fumbled for something to say. Distracted to find nothing, he missed what they said next. When they stopped laughing Stella turned to him as if he had heard.

'This man brings out the worst in me.'

Mr Alfred smiling tried again to find a mite to contribute. By the time he was ready to catch the speaker's eye she was slanted from him, sharing another joke with the man at his elbow. She ended it laughing.

'Aye, I know. The doctor says it's good for you.'

Mr Alfred meditated. Alcohol always made him meditate. His cigarette smouldered at an angle of fortyfive. There was a glow in his middle and a halo round his head. He was getting what he came out to buy. An anaesthetic between the week's drudgery behind and the week's drudgery ahead. Stella was his world for the moment. Stella and what she said and the way she said it. His daily thoughts assured him he was the victim of a coarse and even foul mind. He accepted it, as a redhaired man accepts his red hair. He was willing to believe Stella was never guilty of an equivocation and to blame himself for thinking her conversation was loaded with a wrapped freight of allusions to sexual intercourse. He wondered how he would get on if he tried to make love to her. But he had a good idea what would happen. Even if she ever gave him the chance he would muck it up somehow. He would be sitting an examination in a practical subject when all he had was a little book-learning. He drooped.

When he came out of his soulsearching the man at his elbow was turning to go.

'Good night, sir,' Stella called out, moving up from the other end of the bar to give him a wave.

'You never call me sir,' he said as she came level.

He thought his joking pretence of jealousy would amuse her.

Stella strolled down the bar again and threw him a vague smile over her shoulder. It said she heard him say something but didn't quite know what and didn't think it mattered.

He staggered out on the bell to wintry streets and shivered. Between tall tenements and down dark lanes, his cigarette out, he talked to himself. He criticised the chaste loneliness of his habits. He muttered Milton's question. He had a habit of thinking in quotations when he had a drink on him.

Were it not better done as others use,
To sport with Amaryllis in the shade,
Or with the tangles in Neaera's hair?

When he recited the pleasant alternative suggested by the great puritan poet he remembered an old surmise that *with* should be *withe*, meaning *bind* or *pleat*. It seemed an idea worth lingering over. But at that point in her erotic meditation he was interrupted by a woman who had no resemblance to Amaryllis or any other nymph. She linked her arm in his.

'Coming home, darling?'

He recognised her as the reason for his wandering, and he knew the trembling of his lean body when he left the cosy pub was due less to the chill of a sleety wind than to the hope of finding her. But the moment she opened her mouth and touched him he was as empty as all the glasses he had drained. Still, with his usual politeness he answered insincerely, or with his usual insincerity he answered politely.

'Yes, of course.'

There was a public convenience, doublestaired, a dozen steps ahead. He disengaged his arm from hers with a gentlemanly apology.

'You wait here. I'll be right back.'

He descended, leaving her loitering at the top of the stairs. When he had emptied his bladder he returned to the street by the other staircase and weaved home to his single bed.

THREE

Two of Gerry's classmates collided at playtime. There were about four hundred colts running wild in a small area. Collisions and spills were common. Most often they led to nothing more than a vindictive shove and a corresponding push. But this time Gerry intervened. When the boys began their ritual snarling he jostled them. They tangled. He persuaded one of them to challenge the other. A square-go was fixed for four o'clock in the Weavers Lane. The news of the engagement circulated with a speed only slightly less than the speed of light, which is of course the maximum velocity at which any signal can be communicated in our universe, and Gerry was sure of a big attendance. He sprawled in Mr Alfred's class after playtime, dreamy with pride at being a fight-promoter. He put a pencil between his lips, took it out and exhaled.

'Is that a good cigar?' Mr Alfred asked, very sour.

He was lately finding the afternoons tiring. They sent a jangle of pain round his skull. He felt he was a foreigner trying to get across to people who didn't speak his language. The days when he enjoyed teaching seemed so far away he believed they belonged to somebody else.

Gerry rolled the cylinder between his fingers, tried to squeeze it, sniffed it, looked at it suspiciously.

'Aw sir, it's only a pencil,' he decided.

'Put it away,' said Mr Alfred.

Gerry tapped the end of the pencil on the desk as if he was stubbing a cigarette and set it down with hyperbolic care.

Mr Alfred gave him a hard look. But he had been teaching too long to go looking for trouble. He meant his glare to be enough to show he knew cheek when he saw it and wouldn't take any more.

He glanced at the textbook to check the place and resumed the lesson tabulated there for teacher and pupils. It was, in his opinion, a rather childish exercise in oral composition. But the boys seemed to find it difficult. They hadn't an answer to any question. They sickened him.

'They just sit there pandiculating,' he said to himself. 'Shower.'

From the day Collinsburn became a comprehensive school he had always been given the dullest classes. He resented it. The men who took the bright boys and girls to leaving-certificate level were all honours graduates. But he was sure he was as good as any of them, in spite of the fact he had only an ordinary degree. He was convinced he was better equipped to be Head of the English Department than the man in the job. He had read more widely. He had written prose and verse for the university magazine when he was a student. For a session he had been the magazine's most distinguished poet. He had his collection of unpublished poems behind him, and he kept up with modern poetry. Given the chance he knew he could inspire some good boys in fifth and sixth year with his own abiding love for literature. But the Principal Teacher of English, a portly man prematurely bald and Deputy Head Master, was just a dunce who had never written a poem in his life. He was only a teaching-machine during school hours, and outside them he was a non-smoker and teetotaller who read nothing.

Gerry had no loose change when it came his turn to make a donation to the begging composition. He shrugged, shook his head, and put his pencil-cigar back in his mouth.

Mr Alfred let it pass. He was thinking of the year he had to give up his honours course and settle for an ordinary degree. It was all because his father died suddenly and his mother mourned so much she became a bit unbalanced. He qualified quickly to get a job and bring some money into the house. Then his mother went and died too. If they had only lived another couple of years it would have made all the difference to his status. To his prospects of promotion. To his salary. To the classes he was given.

These cogitations on his misfortune occupied the back of his mind while the front went on soliciting sentences for the oral composition. A yelp from the pubescent anthropoid beside Gerry pulled the emergency cord that stopped both trains. He stared at the startled animal.

'Hey sir, Proven stuck a pin into me.'

'Aw sir, I never,' Gerry declared.

Innocence and indignation sparkled in the young blue eyes.

Mr Alfred walked slowly across the room, stood over them both, glowered down, textbook canted.

'Show me,' he ordered Gerry.

'It's only a safety-pin,' said Gerald.

He opened his fist and showed it.

'It doesn't seem to have been very safe,' said Mr Alfred. 'What were you doing with it?'

'Taking it out my pocket,' said Gerry.

'Why?' said Mr Alfred.

'My braces is broke,' said Gerry. 'I was going to try and sort them.'

'Oh yes?' said Mr Alfred.

'And McLetchie went and shoved his arm into me,' said Gerry. 'You see, I had the pin opened, sir.'

He lolled back, smiling up.

'Wipe that smile off your silly face,' said Mr Alfred.

Gerry raised an open hand to his face and drew it down over his nose and mouth. Took the hand away to reveal a straight face. The bland insolence of the obedience provoked Mr Alfred. He smacked Gerry across the nape. He knew at once he shouldn't have done it. But he damned the consequences. It would soon be time for the peace of a pub-crawl. He sketched an itinerary and wondered if he should go and see Stella again or leave her alone for a bit.

Gerry rubbed the offended neck and drew back from any further attack though none was threatened. Cowering he shouted.

'You're not supposed to use you hands. I'll bring my maw up.'

'Bring your granny too,' said Mr Alfred.

'Ya big messan,' said Gerry.

'You cheeky little rat,' said Mr Alfred, and smacked him again where he had smacked him before.

'I'll tell my maw you called me a rat,' said Gerry.

He crouched over his desk, sullenly puffing the forbidden pencil again.

'Oh, for goodness sake,' said Mr Alfred. 'Take that thing out of your mouth. Anybody would think you were a sucking infant.'

'Oh!' Gerry cried in delight. 'What you said! Wait till I tell my maw.'

FOUR

The Weavers Lane was a good venue for a fight. Not far from the entrance it changed direction sharply, and twenty yards on it veered again before turning to the exit. Whatever went on between the zig and the zag couldn't be seen from either end. To make it still more suitable the centre stretch had a recess of stony soil where some dockens and dandelions maintained a squalid existence.

On one side of the lane: the back walls of Kennedy's soap factory, Mclaren's garage, and Donaldson's paint-works. On the other: the palisade of the railway embankment.

But the fight was a flop. Gerry saw at once where he had gone wrong. He had matched a warmonger with a pacifist. In a minute it was no contest. McKay hit Duthie once, an uppercut wildly off target. Duthie reeled against the spectators. They shoved him back into the ring. He stumbled forward a couple of steps and stopped with his head down and his hands across his face, patiently waiting the next blow. Disgusted at the lack of style in his opponent McKay pushed rather than punched him and Duthie fell down. He lay there. He semed to think he had done his bit and that was the show over. Gerry was annoyed.

'Get up and fight!' he shouted. 'You're yellow!'

To encourage Duthie to rise he kicked him three or four times in the ribs. He made it clear he had a great contempt for Duthie. But Duthie gave no sign of caring about anybody's opinion. He sprawled raniform in defeat and croaked upon an ugly docken. The happy boys and girls, four deep all the way round, jeered at his abjection.

Gerry sighed.

Duthie lay still, waiting and willing for death or the end of the world to come and release him from his agony. Neither event occurred at that particular moment, but his salvation came along in the shape of Granny Lyons, famous locally for the health and vigour of her old age. She used the Weavers

Lane every day as a shortcut between her house and the shops, and she was never one to emulate the Levite if she saw a creature in distress. She broke the ring of fight-fans with a swing of her shopper, hoisted Duthie to his feet, and shook him alive again.

'You stupid wee fool! You should keep out of fights.'

Duthie wept.

'A skelf like you,' Granny Lyons comforted him. 'You're no match for McKay. Oh, I know him all right. And I know that Provan there too. Some bloody widow, that one's mother.'

The dispersed mob reformed at a goodly distance.

'Hey missis!' Gerry called out pleasantly. 'Yer knickers is hingin doon.'

He was hiding behind Jamieson and Crawford, and between the phrases he ducked from a shoulder of the one to an elbow of the other.

Granny Lyons measured them all with blazing eyes.

They retreated under her fire.

'Scum,' said Granny Lyons.

She paused, swinging her shopper, thinking.

'Human rubbish,' she shouted, and went on her way.

Duthie tagged behind her, though it meant he would have to take a detour home.

Gerry's disappointment with the fight stayed with him over teatime until his mother came in. Senga did nothing to make up for it. She obeyed all his orders without a word of complaint. He was a Roman slaveowner defeated by the humility of an early Christian. He tried to make her rebel so that he could batter her. She wouldn't break. She made his tea, kept the fire going, washed the dishes, cleaned his shoes, washed his socks, and switched the TV on and off and on again whenever he told her from the command-post of his armchair. He waited for his mother.

'Big Alfy hit me this afternoon,' he said before she was right in.

'Him again?' said Mrs Provan. 'He's always picking on you, that man.'

'Right across the face,' said Gerald. 'Hard. His big rough hand.'

Mrs Provan threw her handbag on a chair and hurried to him. She took his chin between thumb and forefinger and turned his face left and right, looking for a bruise.

'For nothing?' she asked like one who knows the answer.

'I bet you were giving up cheek,' said Senga unheeded.

'Yes,' said Gerald.

His mother stopped looking. She could see nothing. She was angry.

'I'll see about this. Teachers aren't allowed to use their hand. There's no hamfisted brute going to get away with striking my boy.'

'He called me a rat,' said Gerald. 'And he used a bad word. He said I was a so-and-so-king-infant.'

'Oh, he did, did he?' said Mrs Provan. 'Well, I'll call him worse when I see him. And see him I will. First thing tomorrow. Some teacher him, using that language. You leave it to me, Gerald. You're not an orphan. You've got your mother to protect you.'

FIVE

Granny Lyons had a room-and-kitchen near the prison. It was on the ground floor of the Black Building. She sat knitting by the fire and waited for Mr Alfred. The little clock on the mantelpiece ticked away between Rabbie Burns and Highland Mary. Often he just posted the money, not always with a letter. But once the dark nights came in he called about once a month.

'It's only a couple of days now till Christmas,' she remarked to her needles. 'He'll come tonight.'

He did. In his oldest clothes. A wilted hat on his head, a muffler round his neck, a stained raincoat hiding a jacket that didn't match his trousers, shoes needing to be reheeled.

'You should wear dark glasses too,' she cut at him, 'and finish it.'

He smiled. Her he would always conciliate. He spoke flippantly of his appearance.

'So! You don't like my disguise? But then you never do.'

'No,' she said. 'That's a fact. I never do.'

He saw the china-poet look at his sweetheart. He imagined they were avoiding his eyes in case they let him see they didn't like the way he was dressed.

'You think your boys won't recognise you?' she asked him. 'Sure they'd know you a mile away.'

'Not in the dark,' he answered. 'And I slip round the corner quick.'

'I don't know why you bother at all if you're that ashamed,' she said.

'That's not a nice thing to say. You know perfectly well I'm not ashamed.'

'You should get a transfer to another school. Then nobody here would know you.'

'It's too late for that. It's you should never have come here.'

'I was here before you. It was the only place I could get when I lost the shop. You know that.'

They were both silent then, remembering many things. He spoke first.

'It's quite mild outside tonight.'

'Aye, it's not been bad at all today. For the time of year.'

'The street's very quiet for once.'

'You mean nobody saw you? I think your trouble is you get frightened coming here.'

'I suppose I do. But you know what they'd do if they saw me. Hide in a close and yell after me. Something obscene probably.'

'I had a feeling you'd be round tonight.'

'Well, I thought, seeing it's Christmas. I've brought you something.'

He gave her a bottle of whisky as well as the usual money.

'I know you like your dram', he said.

'Not any more than yourself.'

She poured him a drink. The quantity showed she wasn't a mean woman.

'You have one too,' he said.

'Well, seeing it's Christmas.'

'To my favourite aunt,' he said.

'The only auntie you've got now,' she replied to his toast, unflattered.

'The only one I ever really knew. My mother's favourite sister you were. And it was you helped me when I was a student. Don't think I forget.'

'I had money then I haven't got now.'

'If you need any more you've only to tell me.'

'No, you give me plenty. You shouldn't bother.'

'I promised my mother. Anyway, I owe you it. For the time you paid my fees if nothing else.'

'Well, as I say, I had it then. It was a good shop I had before all that trouble. And there was nobody else to give it to.'

'Is your clock slow?'

'No, it's right. Are you in a hurry?'

'Not particularly.'

'Not particularly? You mean you want to get away round the pubs?'

'I'm not desperate. I was just thinking. It was you gave me my first glass of whisky.'

'I always did my best for you.'

They laughed together.

'I suppose it will be a lot of low dives tonight, in that coat,' she said.

'I suppose so. I like to mix with the common people sometimes. You know, go around incognito.'

He laughed alone.

'You still never think of getting married?' she asked suddenly.

'If a man thinks about it he won't,' he said. 'I mean, you either do or you don't. You don't think about it.'

'You think too much. You should let yourself go. Get a good woman and marry her and get out of those digs you're in.'

'I'm too old for that now.'

'A man's never too old for that.'

'I'm happier away from women,' he said.

He elevated his glass sacramentally and plainchanted.

'The happiest hours that e'er I spent were spent among the glasses-O!'

They communicated in silence after she poured another drink. The little clock went on ticking patiently because there was nothing else it could do. Mr Alfred said into himself the first line of a poem he had lately read, 'The house was quiet and the world was calm'. It called up the small hours when he used to read poetry alone in his room and write little poems for himself. He was taken back, at peace with a glass in his hand and a verse in his head.

From a distance a merry cry rocked in the street. It rode above an advancing babble and rolled under the window.

'Haw, Granny Lyons!'

Repeated.

Chanted loudly, chanted slowly.

'Et ô ces voix d'enfants,' said Mr Alfred, 'chantant dans. . .'

But he was frightened.

'I've been expecting them,' said Granny Lyons.

She was calm. Mr Alfred was shaking. He forgot his whisky. There was an edge on the antiphonal voices now.

'Granny Lyons, ye auld hoor!'

'Sounds like Wilma,' said Granny Lyons.

'Why do they call you granny?' said Mr Alfred, fretting. 'I've never understood that.'

'No idea,' said his aunt, shrugging. 'They always have. Since the day I came here. I've been old witch and old bitch and old granny. Doesn't bother me.'

'Here!' yelled a girl outside. 'Here's your Christmas comming up!'

'Jennifer!' said Granny Lyons. 'Quick!'

She stepped smartly to one side of the window and signalled Mr Alfred to get to the other.

First, a hail of stones against the glass. Next, a long rude ring at the doorbell. Mr Alfred turned to answer it.

'Don't move,' Granny Lyons whispered.

The window imploded. A half-brick landed in the centre of the room bringing glass with it. Then the gallop away of the colts and fillies. The whinnying faded.

Mr Alfred stared dumfouttered at the inexplicable half-brick lying mutely on his aunt's old carpet.

'They're getting worse,' said Granny Lyons.

'Anarchy,' said Mr Alfred. 'Mere anarchy is loosed upon the world. Things fall apart.'

He was pale with fright.

'I chased a crowd of them out the back-close last night,' said Granny Lyons. 'Boys and girls. And still at school most of them.'

'You know who they are?' said Mr Alfred. 'Tell me their names and I'll go to the police.'

'Don't talk soft,' said Granny Lyons. 'Do you think the police would welcome you? What could you prove?'

'But you said you were expecting them. Have they been threatening you?'

'They told me they'd be back. If you can call that a threat. I'm as broadminded as the next person but I'm not putting up with houghmagandy in my back-close.'

'I wish you'd get out of this district,' said Mr Alfred.

'Where could I go? Anyway, it's the same everywhere now.'

'I suppose so,' said Mr Alfred.

'It's my own fault,' she said. 'I ask for it. I should mind my own business. Let them take over. It's their world now. But I never learn. That fight I stopped this afternoon. I should have walked on.'

'What fight?' he asked.

She told him about it while they tacked double sheets of newspaper across the frame of the broken window.

'Some of them were your boys,' she said. 'That big lump Provan was there. One of Wilma's boyfriends.'

'He's kind of young to be anybody's boyfriend,' said Mr Alfred.

'He's her age,' said Granny Lyons. 'She's at your school. Don't you know her? Wilma Beattie.'

'Can't say I do,' said Mr Alfred. 'But then I don't take girls' classes.'

'I've chased the pair of them out that back-close more than once,' said Granny Lyons. 'Ah well! As God made them he matched them!'

SIX

Mrs Provan put on her Sunday coat and went to the school. She saw the headmaster at nine o'clock.

'I'm very angry about this, Mr Briggs,' she said. 'I don't mind anyone chastising my boy if he deserves it. But there's a right way and a wrong way.'

A ruffled hen laying a complaint and making a song about it.

Mr Briggs listened carefully. He was a judicious little man, not long promoted. His brother had recently married a widow on the town council. He was perfectly happy signing the janitor's requisitions and sending instructions round his staff in civil-service English and a neat hand. Other clerical activities were used to keep him from working and allow him a claim he had a lot to do every day. He liked talking to parents because that too occupied his time to the exclusion of less sedentary duties.

Mrs Provan ended her aria in a high note of horror.

'But to slap a boy across the face for nothing! That's something I won't have. No!'

'Ah now come, it couldn't have been for nothing, surely it must have been for something.'

The tenor responded to the soprano, and continued piano.

'I don't mean I condone striking a pupil. Oh no, on the contrary. But on the other hand, I can't believe a man walked up to a boy and suddenly hit him for nothing right out of the blue. I mean to say, it doesn't sound a very likely story. Now does it, Mrs Provan?'

His forearms on the desk, his stainless fingers laced, he leaned forward on his magisterial swivelchair as if he was the Solomon of David's royal blood who had to decide how far maternal affection could influence veracity.

'Surely the boy must have given some provocation,' he coaxed her.

'No, none, I assure you,' said Mrs Provan. 'I have Gerald's word for it. And Gerald never tells lies. He's a good boy.'

'Yes, I'm sure,' said Mr Briggs.

'And even if he did that's not the point,' said Mrs Provan.

'Even if he did?' Mr Briggs looked at her in shocked reproach. 'Did tell lies?'

'Give provocation.' said Mrs Provan. 'A teacher's not supposed to lift his hand to a boy. And to call him a rat, well! As a matter of fact it was worse than that.'

'Oh yes?' said Mr Briggs.

'He used a bad word. He called Gerald a so-and-so rat, not just a rat. Poor Gerald wouldn't even repeat the word. But you and me can guess what he said. I ask you! What kind of language is that for a man supposed to be educated?'

'The question is, what did he say exactly.' said Mr Briggs.

Always discreet he used initials only.

'Did he say a bee rat or an effing rat?'

'An effing rat,' Mrs Provan sent word down from remote control.

'I find it hard to believe,' said Mr Briggs. 'Still, if that's what you say. Leave it with me and I'll speak to the teacher.'

'No, I want to see him myself,' said Mrs Provan. 'I want an apology.'

Mr Briggs tried a weak innoculation of sarcasm.

'In writing?'

It was a mistake. It didn't take.

'Not necessarily,' said Mrs Provan. 'But I insist on seeing him for myself.'

'I'm afraid you can't,' said Mr Briggs. 'I think it would only make things worse. You're too much upset for me to let you see anybody.'

'Of course I'm upset,' said Mrs Provan. 'So would you be upset in my place. I've had to take the morning off my work to come here. It's costing me half a day's wages. Just because of a big bully that's not fit for to be a teacher.'

'You mustn't say things like that,' said Mr Briggs. 'It could land you in trouble. He's fully qualified and very experienced.'

'Aye, so's ma granny,' said Mrs Provan.

Mr Briggs unlaced his fingers and leaned back. He saw no use discussing Mrs Provan's grandmother.

'It broke my heart to come to Tordoch at all,' said Mrs Provan. 'But I couldn't get a house anywhere else. Everybody knows it's the lowest dregs of the city lives down there. But don't you go thinking I'm from a slum like the rest of them because I'm not.'

'Nobody ever said you were,' said Mr Briggs.

He was tired of hearing parents tell him they weren't like the rest of the folk in Tordoch. He was tired of Tordoch and all its inhabitants. Once it was a lovers' walk on the rural margin of the city. Then it became a waste land of bracken and nettles surrounded by a chemical factory, gasworks, a railway workshop and slaghills. At that point the town council took it over for a slum-clearance scheme. They built a barrack of tenements with the best of plumbing and all mod cons and expected a new and higher form of civilisation to flare up by spontaneous combustion.

But the concentration of former slum-tenants in such a bleak site led in a few years to the reappearance of the slum they had left. The first native generation grew up indistinguishable from the first settlers and produced their likeness in large numbers. The fathers had no trade or profession. The mothers were bad managers, and worn out by childbearing they looked fifty when they were barely thirty. The untended children lived a life of petty feuding and thieving, nourished by free milk and free dinners at school when they weren't truanting.

There was a constant shift of population. But there too Gresham's Law operated. The scheme became a pool where sediment settled.

Further out, on the country road, there were half a dozen big houses owned by professional and retired men, and between them and Tordoch proper there were some streets of tidy new villas. Since they had never been part of any housing-scheme these people objected if anyone accused them of living in Tordoch. Regretting the present, they turned to the past. A local historian claimed to have found the name Tordoch in a twelfth-century register of bishopric rents. An amateur etymologist said the name came from the Gaelic *torran*, a hill or knoll, and *dubh* or *dugh*, signifying dark or gloomy, implicitly ascribing a touch of the Gaelic second-sight to those who had first named the place. For now indeed it was a black spot. The police knew it as a nexus of thieves and resettlers.

Mrs Provan wasn't bothered about these matters. She had her own grievance.

'It's the way that man treats Gerald,' she said.

'Like he was dirt. He's got the boy frightened for him, so he has.'

'Oh, I don't think so,' said Mr Briggs.

'I come from a good family,' said Mrs Provan.

'And I rear a good family. And that's without a husband at my back. I'm a hardworking widow I am. Not one of your Tordoch types, neither work nor want.'

'Oh no, I can see that,' said Mr Briggs.

'I'm very angry about this,' said Mrs Provan.

Duet da capo.

He got rid of her after the third time round without letting her see Mr Alfred. He never let a parent see a teacher. He knew it would only end in a slanging match. No teacher could soothe angry mothers the way he could.

By that time it was morning-break. His secretary brought in coffee and a biscuit.

'My goodness, Miss Ancill, is it that time already?' he greeted her.

Over his frugal refreshment, for he never stopped working, he told Miss Ancill what Mrs Provan had said to him and what he had said to Mrs Provan, and while he spoke and drank and nibbled he sorted an accumulation of forms intended for transmission to the Director. Amongst them he saw an application signed A. Ramsay for free meals for his family, six girls and four boys. Against *Occupation* the applicant had written 'unemployed'.

'They're all unemployed round here,' he muttered through his biscuit. 'Unemployed and unemployable.'

'Well, what with the family allowance and benefit it's hardly worth their while,' said Miss Ancill.

'Should be occupation father,' said Mr Briggs, and sipped.

He read the financial statement aloud. Weekly total, twenty one pounds seventeen shillings.

'And they talk about unearned income,' he said.

'It's not the upper ten today have unearned income. It's the layabouts. That's your welfare state for you.'

'Some folk play on it,' said Miss Ancill. 'But you can't just do away with it.'

'Aye, the poor we have always with us,' said Mr Briggs. 'Do you know, there's a child born every two seconds. I read that somewhere the other day.'

'Quite a thought,' said Miss Ancill.

'The trouble here,' he said, 'it's the men of course. They never get a trade. Or even a steady job. They work as vanboys when they leave school, then they're casual labourers. They earn just enough to start courting. Then they marry young and the children come and keep on coming. So the man sits back and stops working. They're not working-class, these people. They're just lumps.'

'You can't stop them marrying,' said Miss Ancill.

Mr Briggs changed the subject.

'Phone the police and tell them I want a policeman for the Ballochmyle Road crossing. The trafficwarden's absent.'

After lunch he reprimanded Mr Alfred for striking a pupil and advised him to be careful what he said in class. Mr Alfred denied he had used bad language, but Mr Briggs had never expected him to admit it. He smiled and nodded and let it pass.

In the afternoon Mrs Duthie came and complained that a boy called Provan had forced her son into a fight and then kicked him when he was down. She had taken the boy to the doctor. The doctor would certify the boy's ribs were all bruises. Mr Briggs said he would speak to Provan about it. He said it was pity she hadn't called at nine o'clock. He would have found that information about Provan useful if he had known it earlier. She said she couldn't have called at nine o'clock because she had a part-time job, mornings only, in the Caballero Restaurant. That led her to tell him about her husband, who hadn't worked for ten years. He was under the doctor on account of his heart. Mr Briggs gave her his sympathy and they parted on excellent terms.

When she had gone he littered his desk with requisitions, class lists, publishers' catalogues, and the unfinished draft of a report on a probationer. He wanted to look busy if anyone came in.

Miss Ancill disturbed him with a cup of tea and a buttered scone. He told her what Mrs Duthie had been saying to him and what he said to her. He was on about the cares and loneliness of office when the bell rang. He hurried out to his car.

Miss Ancill watched him go. She knew all the little jobs that had kept him busy since nine o'clock. She counted them off to the janitor.

'A day in the life of,' she said. 'And the way he blethers to me! It's not a secretary that man wants, it's an audience.'

In the staffroom Mr Alfred raised his voice about the headmaster's bad habit of dealing with parents behind a teacher's back. His colleagues were too eager to get out to listen, and he finished up talking to the soap as he washed his hands.

He was the last to leave. Miss Ancill saw him from her window.

'That poor man,' she said. 'I felt sorry for him today. Briggs had him on the carpet. I think he's getting past it. But still. It's not right. A man like Briggs bossing a man like that. He's so kind and gentle.'

'I think he drinks too much,' said the janitor.

'He needs a woman to take care of him,' said Miss Ancill. 'Did you see the shirt he'd on this morning? Wasn't even fit for a jumble sale.'

'You can't spend your money on drink and buy clothes too,' said the janitor.

SEVEN

Leaving school on a fine spring evening Mr Briggs had to go home by public transport. His car was laid up. There was something wrong with the clutch. He felt devalued. It was a long time since he last stood in a bus-queue with ordinary people, some of whom in this case would be merely assistant teachers on his own staff. He was in a mood to find fault with the universe. Opportunity to let off steam was waiting ahead of him. En route to the bus-stop he passed the Weavers Lane. A fankle of weedy boys loitered there in a state of manifest excitement. Mr Briggs was quick to appreciate the situation. There was something in the wind, and it wasn't the smell of roses. Obviously a fight had been arranged and was due to begin as soon as the coast was clear. The guilt in the shifty eyes of his pupils showed they hadn't expected him to come along. He stopped and scowled. He knew them all. His habit of checking against his index-cards whenever a boy came to his notice had made him familiar with their names, their intelligence quotient, their father's occupation if any, and their address. He knew the good boys from the bad boys, though sometimes he believed the former category was an anomaly, as if one should speak of a square circle.

There they were. All the rascals. A dingy mob in jeans and donkey-jackets. Black, Brown, Gray, Green, White. With McColl, McKay, McKenzie, McPherson. He recognised Taylor, Slater, Wright and Barbour, Baker [and Bourne], Hall [and Knight], Latta [and MacBeath], Liddel [and Scott], Ogilvie [and Albert], Gibson, Holmes, MacDougall and Blackie. A nightmare of classroom names. And lounging blondly, somehow the centre of the shapeless crowd, was Gerald Provan. He grinned, hands in the pockets of his tightarsed jeans, kicking the kerb, radiant with the insolence of an antimath idling out his last term at school.

Sure of his power, speaking in loco parentis, since after all they were barely outside the limits of his bailiwick and the bell releasing them from his jurisdiction had barely ceased vibrating across the gasworks, he demanded the why and wherefore of their hanging about. He waited for an answer. None was offered. Sternly he ordered them to disperse.

'Get home! All of you! At once!'

Curt. Staccato.

Slowly, grudgingly, they went. He stood till they were all on the move.

He went for his bus, pleased with himself. Perhaps the universe wasn't so unjust after all. He wished some of his teachers would learn to put into their voice the same ring of authority as he had done there. The bus was prompt, he got a seat at once, and within half-an-hour he was safe and sound at home. He had a sandstone villa, with garden and garage, outside the city. Over dinner he told Mrs Briggs all the events of his day and what he had done about them.

But no sooner was he round the corner from the Weavers Lane than the scattered boys reassembled. Like birds chased from a kitchen-garden they hadn't flown far.

Last to leave the school, Mr Alfred took the same route to the bus-stop as Mr Briggs. He had lingered longer than usual in the staffroom to give Mr Briggs plenty of time to get away. He always found it a bore having to make conversation on the bus, especially with someone who talked shop as loudly as his headmaster.

When he came to the Weavers Lane he heard a lot of shouting. He stopped and listened. He wasn't even tempted to walk away. He was oldfashioned, and he believed without doubting it was his duty to break up any riotous assembly of schoolboys, whether in school or out of school, during hours or after hours. And anyway he was in no hurry. If he put off time he would be in the city-centre when the pubs were opening. Then he could have one or maybe two before going on to his digs. For the evening he had already planned a route that would take him round some pubs he hadn't been in for a month or so.

He put on a grim face and went deep into the lane. What he saw wasn't a storybook fight with bare fists. It was a battle with studded belts that had once been part of what the army called webbing equipment. His belly fluttered at the madness of it. He was as scared as if he was in there taking part. So excited were the spectators, encouraging Cowan and Turnbull with a good imitation of the Hampden Roar, that Mr Alfred was left standing behind them in the same situation as the three old ladies locked in the lavatory. Nobody knew he was there.

Besides swinging the heavy belt in a highly dangerous

manner Cowan used an unpredictable skill, not without its own vicious grace, in getting inside the range of Turnbull's equally heavy belt and endeavouring to kick his opponent on the testicles.

In one of those attempts he lost his balance, the belt arched from his hand, and he fell unarmed to the ground. The recoil of evasive action brought Turnbull over his prostrate foe. Naturally he kicked him. Then things happened so quickly Mr Alfred was never quite sure what he saw.

It appeared that Gerald Provan moved out of the mob behind Turnbull, raised his knee swiftly in a poplitic nudge, sent Turnbull sprawling beside Cowan. The two fighters scrambled up clinching. They wrestled into the crowd, and the crowd pushed them back into the ring. In that surge and sway Gerald Provan thrust a knife into Cowan's hand and then shoved him off to continue the duel.

At that point Mr Alfred broke out of his paralysis. Partly he had been curious to see just what the two boys would do, partly he was afraid of raising his voice too soon and not being heard above the howling of the fans. But when it was seen that Cowan had a knife there was a breathless hush in the lane that night and Mr Alfred knew his moment was come. Cowan lunged, Turnbull dodged, and Mr Alfred spoke out loud and clear.

'Stop that!'

His voice scattered most of the onlookers. They had no wish to be involved. Turnbull froze. Cowan threw the knife away and with coincident speed dissolved into the melting crowd. Provan tried to make a quick getaway by diving behind Mr Alfred. It was a blunder. Mr Alfred caught him on the turn and held him by the collar. Gerald wriggled.

'Hey, mind ma jacket, you! Ma clothes cost good money, no' like yours.'

Mr Alfred shook him and threw him away.

'I'll see you tomorrow,' he said.

He saw the knife lying on top of a docken on the margin of the arena. He picked it up and put it in his pocket. He thought it was evidence.

EIGHT

It must not be supposed that the boys and girls gathered in the Weavers Lane that night were a fair representation of the pupils attending Collinsburn Comprehensive, the only school in Tordoch for post-primary education. Collinsburn was a local place-name, derived from the legend that a stream once ran through that part of Tordoch formerly owned by a Collins family whose members, like the vanished burn, had long gone underground. As a comprehensive school Collinsburn harboured all kinds and ages [mental and chronological]. So while Mr Alfred was shaking Gerald Provan, Graeme Roy was sitting with Martha Weipers in Ianello's cafe round the corner from the main road. It was a roomy, almost barnlike place, that sold cigarettes and sweets and ices and offered half-a-dozen stalls where the young ones could sit with a coffee or a coke and criticise the world.

Graeme Roy was eighteen, in his last year at school. Martha was a year younger and not as clever as he was. At least, that's what she thought. She even found pleasure in believing it. They should have gone straight home, but they had got into the habit of using Ianello's for half-an-hour.

They were under parental orders to stop meeting. Their daily sessions in the cafe after school gave them the satisfaction of at once obeying and ignoring the order. They no longer met in the evenings, so they were obedient. But they still managed to meet for a little while on the way home, so they evaded the full severity of the law.

She was the poor one, the eldest of seven, a bricklayer's daughter. He was an only son and well-off, a handsome youth. He had a driving-licence and a car of his own. He used to take Martha out for a run in the summer evenings after the exams were over. When the quartet of parents found out what was going on they slammed down hard on the pair of them. Graeme's folks had never thought he was taking a girl out when he used his car, and Martha's had no idea she had a rich boyfriend. Nasty suspicions were aroused, some accusations were made that hurt and even shocked them, and then the forthright veto was proclaimed.

Without collusion, without ever meeting, the two sets of parents reacted in the same way and came to the same conclusion. His parents said only a girl with no self-respect would accept an invitation to go out alone with a boy in his car. Her parents said no decent right-thinking boy would ask a girl to come out alone with him in his car. Unless of course, both sides conceded independently, the boy and girl were engaged. Which would be absurd at their age. Further meetings, with or without the car, were bilaterally banned. It was for their own good their parents said.

'They try to tell us we're too young,' he said.

'That's how they see it,' she said. She was a fairminded girl. 'They're so old. My dad's nearly forty.'

'But that's not the real reason,' he said. 'It's my mother. I hate to say it. But she's an awful snob. She thinks because your father works with his hands I shouldn't talk to you. I told her a surgeon works with his hands, but she wouldn't listen.'

'My dad's the same,' she said. 'He won't listen. He thinks if folks are well-off they must be on the fiddle. Because your father's got a car and could buy you one too my dad's sure he's a crook.'

'Oh, my father's honest enough,' he said. 'He wouldn't cheat anybody.'

'My dad would cheat anybody for five bob,' she said. 'For all his supposed principles. That's the funny thing.'

'My dad wouldn't,' he said. 'But then five bob's nothing to him. It's my mother's the trouble. She's hard. A lot harder than my father. It's my mother I blame.'

'My mother doesn't count in our house.' she said, and added with a young laugh, 'she doesn't read either.'

He smiled. He was happy. He liked to see her laugh when she was with him. He didn't like it when he saw her laugh in any other company.

They got on well. They never had any difficulty talking. There were never any silences. They tore their parents to bits, and put the bits together again with the quick adhesive of filial tolerance. They were two earnest adolescents, able to vary their solemn dialogue with a private joke. They had the same liking for the depreciatory aside, the same bias on current affairs, the same cynical tone when they talked about their teachers. Never before, in all their long experience, had they felt such affinity with anyone else.

The first time she met him he liked her. It was at the inaugural meeting of the Debating Society. Mr Briggs had started it with a view to entering a team in an annual inter-schools debate. There was a big silver cup for the winning school and a plaque for the runners-up, and he thought either would look rather well beside the football trophies in the display cabinet at the Main Entrance. Maisie Munro, a beaming jumbo of a girl with glasses, who lived near Graeme, introduced them. She was a prefect in Martha's class.

'This is Graeme,' she said. 'You know, the famous Roy.'

He was famous at that time because he had scored a goal that put Collinsburn into the semi-final of the City Cup, but Martha didn't know that. She had no interest in football.

'Tell me,' she said when Maisie left them stuck alone together in a corner, 'is your name Graham Roy or Roy Graham?'

'Not Graham,' he said. 'Graeme.'

He made one syllable where she made two. Her speech was looser than his. She was more Scotch, he was more anglified. She was apt to say fillim for film, to make no distinction between hire and higher. She could even insert a neutral vowel between the two consonants at the end of warm and learn and such words. It was the way she trilled the r made her do it. Sometimes it offended his ear, but his heart didn't mind.

'Graeme,' he repeated to her stare. 'Not Graham.'

'However you say it,' she retorted, 'you still haven't said if it's your first name or your second.'

She wasn't put out by his correction. Far from it. She was amused. He was so tidy, trim, well-dressed and superior, and spoke so correctly.

Her levity pleased him. He explained. His father's name was John Barbour Roy, his mother's name was Alison McKenzie Graeme. They had the equalitarian idea of calling him Graeme Roy, so that each would contribute their share to his name as they had already done to his existence. Later on, when he knew her better, he confessed that his mother's name was really Graham but she thought Graeme was a more stylish version.

From the night they met at the Debating Society he began to look out for her and she looked out for him looking out for her. They grew in affection with the growing season. He had to tell her everything. He wasn't boasting. He just had to tell her. He didn't want to hide anything. He told her his father was a director in an engineering firm, he told her his mother was the graduate daughter of a defunct Conservative M.P. He described the big house where he lived. It was in an old-world residential outpost, an Edwardian if not Victorian survival from the days when Tordoch was still rural. His parents weren't happy to have him attending Collinsburn. They regretted not moving him to a fee-paying school in the west end when Collinsburn changed from a local Academy to a regional Comprehensive. But he was so near his exams for university entrance it seemed best to leave him where he was.

He mentioned one of his mother's complaints. She was brought up in a house with a maid that lived in, and now she couldn't get anything better in her own house than an unreliable daily-help, a dismal widow who scamped the work.

In class-conscious retaliation Martha gave him an account of her domestic troubles. She had to do it all herself.

'It's worst in the winter. I'm up at six in the morning. Oh my, oh my, it's that cold! And it's that dark! I've to get the fire lit and start making my dad's porridge and give him a shout but he won't get up till I've got the fire going. Then when I've got rid of him I get my three young sisters up and make their breakfast and while they're taking their cornflakes I get my two wee brothers up and after I've got them dressed and fed and got them ready for school I get Jean up and wash her and dress her. Jean's only three. And by that time I've got to get myself ready for school.'

'But what's your mother doing?' he asked.

'She stays in bed till I take her a cup of tea before I go out,' said Martha. 'She's a poor soul really. She doesn't keep well. She gets up when we're all away and looks after Jean.'

He brimmed with pity and fell in love.

But let's have no misunderstanding. Although she was Martha and not Mary she never felt sorry for herself. She never saw herself as Martha in Beth-ania, the House of Care. She was no spiritless drudge, no pallid, thinlegged, flatchested, dullfaced little skivvy, but a lively, chatty, slim, brighteyed, clearskinned young blonde, promising at seventeen to be what blondes are vulgarly supposed to be anyway, that is, lushus–if she lived long enough.

'It must be interesting,' he said, not quite insincerely. 'Being one of a big family.'

'It's a bit of a bind at times,' she said. 'You never get any peace. You're never alone. I'd love to be alone once in a while.'

They were sitting there in Ianello's, quite content, with a coffee in front of them. Sometimes their hands touched across the table as they spoke, but they never actually held hands. He made no show of affection in public, nor did she. They despised teenagers that did. They considered themselves older, more mature.

Their conversation was disturbed by the loud entrance of Gerald Provan and his company.

'See me in the morning, says he,' Gerald was shouting as he came in. 'I'll fix him, the auld grey bastard! I'll get ma maw on to him again. She sorted him last time all right.'

'Oh dear,' said Martha.

'What are you laughing at, Poggy?' said Gerald. 'Think I'm feart for him?'

'Ach, him!' Poggy shouted, shoulder to shoulder with him at the counter. 'Who's feart for him? It's a kick on the balls he needs.'

He was a big lad, Gerald's loyal bondman.

Enrico Ianello came flustered from the backshop, fluttered at them, wanting peace and quiet, good business with decorum. His parents had left Naples with similar ambitions for the unattainable. He was a smallish man, plump, darkeyed, darkskinned, a bit of a singer when he was in the mood. He had a good moustache and a double chin. Mr

Alfred said he looked like Balzac. Granny Lyons had never seen Balzac, but she liked Enrico and hoped her nephew was being kind.

'Where's Smudge?' Gerald called out, turning round to face his followers.

'They didn't use to come here,' Graeme whispered.

A thin little swarthy miasmal wraith of a boy joined Gerald at the counter.

'Here, boss,' he grinned. His teeth were yellow and deficient.

'Good lad,' said Gerald.

'Did you see him pick up the knife?' Smudge shouted.

'They're taking over,' said Martha.

'I bet you he tries to say it was me had it,' Gerald shouted back.

'You'd think they were across the street from each other, the way they shout,' said Graeme.

'I'll say you never,' Poggy shouted. 'Don't worry, pal.'

'Let's get outa here,' said Martha. 'As they say on those old fillims on the telly.'

They rose at once together. They were always en rapport. They went out, backed by a medley of jeering farewells from their comprehensive juniors.

'Ta-ta, toffee-nose.'

'Wur we annoying you, blondie?'

'Gie us a wee kiss, sugar-lumps!'

Poggy knew her name. He jumped, waving to her.

'Hey, Martha Weipers! If I get a car will ye come oot wi me?'

She went red in the face.

'Hoy! Windscreen-wipers! D'ye no hear me?'

Graeme held the door open, head up, and handed her out.

They stood a while fretting at the bus-stop where Mr Briggs had waited half-an-hour earlier.

'I'm not going back there,' she said. 'It's getting worse.'

'Where else can we go?' he asked.

'I don't know. But don't ask me to go back there.'

She looked so upset he made up his mind to persuade her to meet him at night as she used to do.

It probably doesn't matter, but in case you think this is all made up here are the names and ages of Martha's brothers and sisters. ['The bricks are alive at this day to testify it; therefore deny it not.']

Mary, 15.

Rose, 12 [who has her own place in this true narrative, and of whom Martha once said to Graeme, 'She's a bit dopey. Dreamy I mean. I don't think she'll ever be a great scholar. But she's quite pretty. And awfully good-natured. Do anything for anybody.'].

Christine, 10.

Angus, 8.

Billy, 6.

Jean, 3.

Martha looked after them all. Her mother was married at twentytwo, so she was thirtysix when Jean was born. She wasn't an unintelligent woman, but bearing seven children had sapped her strength, rearing them had narrowed her mind, and the hard years had discouraged her. Sometimes she felt life wasn't worth the living.

Martha's father was a big strong man who liked work and beer. He had a lot of commonsense about everything in general and anything in particular. He was very fond of Martha but he never showed it. He thought it wouldn't be decent for a man his age to embrace a girl of seventeen, so he treated her with a cold obliquity. He ignored Mary because she was at a gawky age and made a favourite of Rose.

NINE

The teachers in Collinsburn used corporal punishment. Every time somebody wrote to the papers about the wrongness of it they laughed in the staffroom and agreed about the rightness of it. An English immigrant's letter complaining about the place of the tawse in Scottish education set them off again.

'The way these folk talk,' said Mr Brown, Deputy Head and Principal Teacher of English, 'you'd think we spent our whole day belting defenceless weans.'

'You give some pest one of the strap to keep him in line,' said Mr Campbell, Principal Teacher of Mathematics, 'and they call it corporal punishment.'

'Then in the next sentence it becomes flogging,' said the Principal Teacher of Modern Languages, Mr Kerr.

He read aloud from the offensive letter.

'Hyperbole,' said Mr Brown.

'They think we're a shower of bloody sadists,' said Mr Dale, the youngest member of staff. 'They've no idea.'

'The strap is only a convention here,' said Mr Campbell. 'Up to second year anyway. You don't need it much after that. But if you abolished it altogether you'd raise more problems than you solved.'

'It's like the language of a country,' said Mr Alfred from his lonely corner. 'You've got to speak it to be understood.'

His colleagues hushed and looked at him. He seldom opened his mouth during their discussions. He seemed to think himself above them. They were surprised to hear his voice.

Mr Alfred acknowledged their attention by taking his cigarette out of his mouth. He went on chattily as if he was giving a reminiscent talk on the Light Programme.

'I remember one school I worked in. There was a young Latin teacher next door to me. Very young he was. He wouldn't use the strap he told me. He thought the language of the strap was a barbaric language. He would speak to the natives in his own civilised tongue. He would be all sweetness and light like Matthew Arnold.'

'Hear, hear!' cried Mr Dale.

'Bloody fool,' muttered Mr Brown.

Mr Alfred smiled agreeably to them both and continued his talk.

'But when the natives found he refused to speak their language their pride was hurt. They felt he was insulting their tribal customs. They regarded him as a mad foreigner. They sniped at him till they saw it was safe to make an open attack. Within a week they were making his life hell on earth.'

'Boys can be cruel to a weak teacher,' said Mr Campbell.

'He was baited and barbed,' said Mr Alfred.

'By defenceless children,' said Mr Brown.

'Until he broke under the torture,' said Mr Alfred.

'Once they think you're soft they've no mercy,' said Mr Kerr.

'He went berserk one day,' said Mr Alfred. 'He thrashed a boy across the legs and buttocks and shoulders with the very strap he had wanted to put into a museum.'

'Probably the least troublesome boy,' said Mr Campbell.

'It usually is,' said Mr Kerr.

'It was,' said Mr Alfred. 'I heard the row. I heard the boy run screaming from the room as if the devil were after him. I nipped out in time to catch him in the corridor and managed to pacify him. I took him to the toilets and had him wash his face and calm down. I like to think I stopped what could have been a serious complaint from the parent.'

'It would never have happened if he had used the strap just once the day he arrived,' said Mr Campbell.

'Precisely my point,' said Mr Alfred.

'I always let a new class see I've got a strap and let them know I'll use it,' said Mr Dale. 'After that I've no bother. If you show the flag you don't need to fire the guns.'

'And you know,' said Mr Alfred, 'the tawse of the Scotch dominie is never wielded like the Jesuit's pandybat that distressed the young Stephen Dedalus. Not that the pandybat did Joyce any harm. It gave him material. It showed him what life is like. These letterwriters would have us deceive the boys by pretending they'll never be punished later on in life when they do something wrong. And even if a boy is strapped unjustly it isn't fatal. Life is full of minor injustices. A boy should learn as much while he's still at school, and learn to take it without whining. I admire the heroes of history who fought against social injustice, but one of the strap given in error or loss of patience is hardly a wrong on that scale.'

He put his cigarette back in his mouth and withdrew from the discussion. He thought he had said all that needed saying about corporal punishment.

'The way I see it,' said Mr Campbell, 'the strap is our symbol of authority within a recognised code. The boys know what to expect and we can get on with the job.'

'You must have something to maintain discipline,' said Mr Kerr. 'Some quick sanction. Even if you never use it.'

'No discipline, no learning,' said Mr Brown.

'But tell me this,' said Mr Dale. 'What do you do if a boy refuses to take the strap?'

'Only a stupid teacher would create a situation where that would happen,' said Mr Campbell.

'But supposing,' said Mr Dale.

'It's a case for the headmaster then,' said Mr Brown.

'I've never met many cases of a boy refusing the strap,' said Mr Campbell. 'And those I have, they all came to nothing. The boy had to submit in the end and apologise. Then of course once he gets a public apology the teacher acts the big man. He won't condescend to strap the boy. The rebel ends up looking a bit of an ass.'

'Well, I'm deputy-boss here,' said Mr Brown, 'and I've never had any boy refuse the strap. We don't seem to get that kind of stupid defiance.'

So it was an occasion for headlines when Gerald defied Mr Alfred and kept on defying him the morning after the fight in the Weavers Lane.

Before proposing to strap him Mr Alfred told the class what he had seen in the Weavers Lane. He said those who egged boys on to fight were worse than the boys who came to blows. Even a good boy might get into a fight if he thought his honour was at stake. He would fight in case his classmates jeered at him if he didn't. That was silly. Nothing was ever solved by violence. Still, it was a pardonable mistake in a young person. But few boys would fight at all if nobody talked them into thinking they had to. This was usually done by trouble-makers who took jolly good care never to risk their own precious skin. It was a far, far better thing to tell your schoolmates there was no need to fight. Our saviour said, Blessed are the peacemakers. The really wicked ones were those who were not content to start two boys fighting with their bare fists but got them to use belts and even brought a knife into it. They were not blessed like the peacemakers. They deserved a deep damnation more than a ticking off.

He spoke very well and enjoyed having the class hushed at his rhetoric. Then he said quietly, 'Come out Gerald Provan.'

He raised his strap.

'You know what I've been talking about. You know why I'm going to punish you.'

Gerald refused to hold his hand out. He said he had done nothing wrong, it was after four o'clock when he was in the Weavers Lane, Mr Alfred had no right, he was picking on him. He spoke with a rough insolence. His tongue darted between his lips and he went through the motion of spitting at Mr Alfred's feet.

Mr Alfred nearly slapped him across the face there and then. But he saw the trap.If he let himself be provoked and hit Gerald with his hand he would put himself in the wrong. His case against Gerald would be obliterated by Gerald's case against him. He knew he had blundered. He should have referred the whole business to Mr Briggs. And he was uneasy to think it was just possible he had jumped at the chance to get at Gerald Provan because he didn't like the boy. It vexed him even more that now he would have to take the matter to Mr Briggs not as something he was merely reporting but something he had failed to handle.

The class watched his defeat with placid interest.

He grabbed Gerald by the scruff and pushed him to the door.

'You come and see the headmaster,' he said.

'Take your hauns aff me,' said Gerald.

His dialect vowels were themselves a form of insolence. Normally a boy spoke to his teacher in standard English.

Mr Briggs wasn't pleased when Mr Alfred shoved Gerald in and said his piece. But he could only support his teacher. He ordered Gerald to take his punishment. He said he was sick and tired of all the feuding and fighting that was going on in the school and he was determined to stamp it out. He nearly said with a firm hand. He said he himself had told all those boys in the Weavers Lane to go home at once. If for nothing else, Gerald deserved to be punished for disobeying that order. Mr Alfred was quite right to strap him. He would do it himself if Mr Alfred wouldn't. And in order that justice would not only be done but be seen to be done, Mr Alfred or he himself would strap Gerald in front of the whole class.

Gerald was stubborn. He said Mr Alfred had a spite at him. He wouldn't take the strap from him. And he wouldn't take the strap from Mr Briggs. It was the same thing. Whoever did it, he was still being strapped for nothing. He put his hands behind his back. No, he wouldn't take it.

He had worked himself into a mood and he was stuck with it. But he was thrilled with the stand he was making. He knew his cause was just.

'Here's the knife I told you about,' said Mr Alfred.

He put it on the headmaster's desk.

Mr Briggs glanced at it, wrinkled his nose and looked away. He didn't touch it.

'It's not mines,' said Gerald. 'I've got witnesses.'

'Mine,' said Mr Alfred.

'We're not discussing that,' said Mr Briggs. He lolled back in his swivel chair, looking at his clean nails. 'That will come later. At the moment all I'm concerned with is you were one of the boys in the Weavers Lane and you returned after I had sent you all away. You'll either take your punishment for disobedience or you'll go home and tell your mother I want to see her.'

The option was his final bluff. Ninetynine times out of a hundred a boy capitulated rather than bother his parents. This time it failed. Gerald went home at once. He even banged the door on his way out.

'You should never have tried to strap him just for watching a fight,' Mr Briggs scolded Mr Alfred. 'You know what he's like. And his mother's worse. The knife? That won't get us anywhere. It's just your word. He'll deny it. If you had only sent him to me in the first place I could maybe have talked him into taking the strap. Even if he had defied me it wouldn't have been in front of a class. That won't do you any good with the rest of them, you know. I could have got round it somehow if it had been kept in this room. But now God knows what we've started.'

TEN

Before the week was out he found he had started plenty. Gerald turned up the next day, early and unworried. Mr Briggs spotted the fair hair in the assembly and beckoned.

'Where's your mother?'

He waited.

Gerald said nothing.

'Go away,' said Mr Briggs, 'and don't come back here without her.'

Mrs Provan came to his room at nine o'clock the following morning with Gerald by her side, her hand on his shoulder. She was angry again. She said her boy hadn't taken part in any fight. The truth was he had done his best to stop a fight. He had even brought one of the boys home with him and used his hankie to stench the blood flowing from the boy's nose where a big bully had punched him.

'I can show you the hankie,' she said.

'And I can show you a knife,' said Mr Briggs. 'It's not just a penknife. It's more like a dagger. Just look at it. Do you allow your boy to go around with a thing like that in his pocket?'

'No, and I don't allow him to tell lies either,' said Mrs Provan. 'That's not his knife. He told you so himself.'

'Mr Alfred saw him with it,' said Mr Briggs.

'That's his story,' said Mrs Provan. 'Gerald never had a knife like that in his life. I should know. I'm his mother. Not Mr Alfred.'

'All I'm asking,' said Mr Briggs, 'is for Gerald to take the strap. There's no question of severe punishment. If he'll take even one. It won't kill him.'

'I never said it would,' said Mrs Provan. 'I'm only saying you're not strapping my boy for nothing.'

'I've got to think of the discipline of my school,' said Mr Briggs. 'The boy disobeyed an order from me in the first place. I can't just ignore it.'

'That was after school,' said Mrs Provan. 'It had nothing to do with you.'

'He also disobeyed Mr Alfred. In the classroom. Not after school.'

'Aye, but it was about something that happened after school,' said Mrs Provan. 'And that man has a spite against Gerald.'

She wouldn't give in. Mr Briggs said if the boy wouldn't accept the laws of the school he had no option but to suspend him. He told her to think it over and sent them both away.

'I've no need to think it over,' said Mrs Provan at the door. I'll be back here tomorrow. It's you had better think it over. I know my rights. You'll take my boy in if you're wise. You've no authority to keep him out.'

'Oh but I have,' said Mr Briggs.

'That's two days now he hasn't had his milk,' said Mrs Provan. 'He's got a right to his free milk every day. It's laid down by the law of the land. Lucky for you you didn't stop him getting his dinner here yesterday.'

'I didn't see him or I would have stopped him,' said Mr Briggs.

'He's got a ticket for free meals,' said Mrs Provan. 'I'm a widow woman. I applied for free meals for my children and it was granted. You can't stop it.'

'I can,' said Mr Briggs. 'In certain circumstances.'

'That's what you think,' said Mrs Provan. 'I know different. Not to mention the fact he's missed his education for two days through your fault.'

'Education! For that fellow!' Mr Briggs cried to Miss Ancill, giving her a line by line account of the interview over his morning coffee. 'He leaves in a couple of months. He's hardly a candidate to stay on for O levels. He has learned all he'll ever learn at school. And God knows that wasn't much.'

When Mrs Provan brought Gerald back again he offered her a compromise. He wouldn't punish the boy nor would

Mr Alfred, if she would concede they had a right to punish him.

'Not for doing nothing,' said Mrs Provan.

The peace talks broke down. Mr Briggs told her to come back when she changed her mind.

She didn't. She wouldn't. She phoned the fourth estate. She knew enough to know a free press is the guarantee of liberty. Within twenty-four hours a counter-attack was organised. Gerald arrived at school in a Ford Anglia driven by a bearded reporter accompanied by a bald photographer. He got out at the gate and went straight to Mr Briggs' room while his escorts waited in the playground. Five minutes after he sauntered out smiling. The photographer had a word with him and then took his picture against the wall of the boys' urinal. By an unfortunate coincidence Mr Alfred came along at that moment. He slowed down when he saw Gerald being photographed by a bareheaded man in a sheepskin coat and saw another man, similarly clad, shepherding a jolly crowd of pupils out of the picture. He was puzzled.

'That's him,' Gerald whispered.

The man with the camera turned quickly. Mr Alfred gaped. The man with the beard stepped forward.

'Good morning, sir,' he said pleasantly. 'Would you give me your views on corporal punishment?'

The man with the camera took aim.

Mr Alfred looked round for escape. He was jostled by cheering boys and girls and confronted by this bearded stranger with the big smile and the unexpected question. He faced him fiercely, glare answering grin.

The man with the camera snapped.

'Thank you,' he sang out.

'Excuse me,' said Mr Alfred, and barged on.

When the evening paper came out there wasn't only Gerald full length on the front page. Mr Alfred was there too, head and shoulders. A single column story under a three column headline separated the two pictures. The headline was *Teacher Has Spite Says Mum*.

Mr Brown brought in a copy next morning in case Mr Alfred had missed it.

'You look a right badtempered old bastard there,' he said.

Mr Alfred hadn't seen his picture. He seldom bought an evening paper. He was shocked. He had the same irrational disbelief as some people have when they hear their voice on tape for the first time. That wasn't him. To increase the offence, Gerald looked boyish and handsome, happy and innocent.

'Crabbed age and youth,' said Mr Brown.

'That face doesn't do our image any good, does it?' said Mr Dale.

Mr Alfred drank more than usual that night. He went on a pub-crawl in what Granny Lyons called his disguise, but he was sure everybody recognised him. He couldn't forget how his face looked in the paper. And that would be how it looked to other people he supposed. Yet he knew he had once been tall, dark and handsome, with a profile and a moustache that made his fellow students say he looked like Robert Louis Stevenson.

When he got back to his lodgings he hunted out the typescript of his poems. It was a long time since he last looked at them. He had an alcoholic whim to read them again and enter the mind of the man he had been in the green years that had no ophidian Provan lurking in the grass. He thought he would comfort his troubled spirit by saying his own verses aloud.

He had called his poems *Negotiations for a Treaty*. He meant a treaty with the reality of philosophers, politicians, economists, scientists and businessmen. The thirty-two poems he had typed in a fair copy after countless revisions were meant to be a lyric-sequence showing the attempt to come to terms with a material world. The poet would insist on his right to live in the independent republic of his imagination. But he would let reality be boss in its territory if it gave up all claims to invade and conquer his. If it didn't he would organise his own resistance movement.

The performance fell short of the intention. He was depressed to see how weak and derivative his verses sounded after lying long unread. He felt he was a failure, a lonely provincial hearing from afar rumours of the world of letters, the only world he cared about, a world he would never be allowed to enter. And he saw his failure didn't come from an addiction to drink and idleness. It came from the whole cast and calibre of his mind. Sleep seemed impossible. He wished he had taken just one more whisky at the bar before it closed, or bought a half-bottle to carry out so that he could have another drink before he went to bed.

Undressing slowly he saw himself as a man tossed aside by a God who had given him the ambition to be a poet without giving him the talent.

Mr Briggs saw him as a bit of a fool who had brought unnecessary publicity to the school by mishandling a difficult boy. The evening paper that started the story followed it up for a week. So did the morning paper that was its stable companion. There was *Mother Demands Enquiry* on the front page with a picture of Gerald and Mrs Provan cheek to cheek like sweethearts. Then there was *Banned Boy Tries Again* on the middle page with a picture of Gerald at the school gate, like Adam outside the gates of Paradise, wearing his best suit, face washed and hair combed. But at the week-end a youth was stabbed to death in a brawl outside a dance-hall in Sauchiehall Street. His griefstricken girlfriend was a photogenic blonde who was interviewed on her thoughts about life and love. She displaced Gerald and his mother.

ELEVEN

Although the Provan story was no longer newsworthy the papers went on drawing dividends from it. Letters to the Editor condemning corporal punishment were printed daily for several weeks and filled a lot of space. They appeared most frequently and at the greatest length in the *Herald*.

'More letters this morning!' cried Mr Brown.

He breezed in waving his paper.

'Hey, shut that door, there's a draught,' said Mr Campbell. A cross man.

'A long one from Monica Trumbell,' said Mr Brown.

He slammed the door with a backheeler and pitched an eager question at Mr Alfred:

'Have you seen it?'

Mr Alfred stooped at the staffroom table sipping a cup of strong tea brewed by a kindly cleaner forty minutes before the first of the staff arrived.

'No,' he said. 'Who is Monica, what is she?'

'One of our conquerors,' said Mr Dale. 'She's up here on loan from England.'

'She damn near names you as the villain of the piece,' said Mr Brown.

'Oh yes,' said Mr Alfred.

He sipped his tea.

Mr Brown read to him with loud gusto.

'"It is a sorry comment on Scottish education when some survivor from a prehistoric society thinks he can solve the most subtle problems of school discipline by resorting to brute force against a sensitive adolescent."'

'An excess of sibilants surely,' said Mr Alfred.

'Onomatopoeia,' said Mr Brown. 'She's hissing you.'

'Who is she, I was asking,' said Alfred.

'Monica Trumbell?' said Mr Campbell. He frowned a moment, then identified a function. 'That's that dame is always writing letters. She's the secretary of POISE, isn't she?'

'That's the one,' said Mr Dale. 'A poisonality.'

'What is poise, saith my sufferings then?' Mr Alfred enquired.

'POISE?' said Mr Brown. 'You mean to say you don't know what POISE is?'

'Not as something having a secretary,' said Mr Alfred.

'It's an acronym,' said Mr Brown. 'It stands for Parents' Organisation for the Improvement of Scottish Education. You're not keeping up! It's old models like you POISE is out to improve on.'

'There's always room for improvement,' said Mr Alfred.

He sipped his tea and glanced at the electric clock on the wall. Two minutes to the bell. He sipped his tea again.

'She's good, our Monica,' said Mr Dale. 'Mrs Monica actually. Oh Jaysus, I'd hate to sleep with her. I bet she'd tell you your way of doing it was out-of-date.'

'How is she qualified to improve anybody?' Mr Alfred asked. 'Except herself of course.'

'I told you,' said Mr Dale. 'She's English.'

'Oh I see,' said Mr Alfred.

He sipped his tea, squinting over the rim of the cup at the sinister clock.

'She's married to the personnel boss at Bunter's Ball Bearings,' said Mr Dale. 'You know, the English firm that came to the new Salthill industrial scheme. A shower of Sassenachs out there now.'

'She's from Essex actually,' said Mr Brown.

'Upminster. Here about a year. The *Herald* had an article on her last week.'

'Oh yes,' said Mr Alfred.

'On the Woman's Page,' said Mr Brown.

'Complete with picture,' said Mr Dale. 'A horsefaced old haybag.'

'A reformer,' said Mr Campbell. 'The minute she sees a pie she shoves her finger in.'

'She's got two girls at Bay,' said Mr Brown.

'Two girls at bay,' Mr Alfred turned gladly. 'I thought it was stags one had at bay.'

'Bay School,' said Mr Campbell.

'Private school for girls,' said Mr Brown.

'You couldn't send your daughter there,' said Mr Dale.

'I know,' said Mr Alfred. 'I haven't got a daughter. Not as far as I know.'

'If you had you couldn't,' said Mr Campbell. 'Not on your salary.'

'It's not a school,' said Mr Dale. 'It's an advance post of English infiltration. Hockey and an English accent. The old girl network.'

Mr Alfred glanced at the clock. The bell rang.

He swallowed the last of his tea and was first out to meet his class.

At morning break Mr Brown was still in a teasing mood. He read out further extracts from Mrs Trumbell's letter and bits from a letter supporting her. Mr Alfred wasn't amused. Mr Brown's voice jarred on him and he disliked the man's use of juvenile slang. He tried to show his disapproval by sighs and groans but Mr Brown wasn't discouraged.

'Here's a smashing argument,' he declared loud and clear.

'Must you?' Mr Alfred asked.

Mr Brown read with zest to his jaded colleagues.

'"It is surely obvious to the meanest intelligence, even amongst teachers—"'

Mr Campbell was jolted from his crossword.

'That bloody cheek!' he cried. '"Even amongst teachers!"'

'Than whom,' said Mr Alfred.

Mr Brown read straight on through the interruptions.

'"–that a pupil refuses punishment because he is the innocent victim of certain psychical and physical strains resulting in a feeling of resentment due to his immaturity. Now whatever the child resents cannot be just and should therefore be abolished."'

'Hear, hear,' said Mr Dale. 'Let's abolish the weans as well. That'll solve it.'

Mr Brown laughed and continued.

'"This applies particularly to that curse of Scottish education, corporal punishment. Not that way will the child with a thirst for knowledge be provided with a key to wider horizons."'

'Oh ma Goad!' said Mr Dale.

'She'll be leaving no stone unturned till she nips us in the bud,' said Mr Campbell.

Mr Alfred sighed and groaned again. Mr Brown continued.

'"A system of sanctions must be devised which will not produce resentment in the child. Here is a task for our child-psychologists. Meanwhile in view of the present atmosphere of frustration which is itself an indication of a great deterioration in our much-vaunted determination to create a higher civilisation I appeal to parents of every denomination to send me their application for registration in the Parents Organisation for the Improvement of Scottish Education."'

'Damnation,' said Mr Alfred.

'Listen to this,' said Mr Brown. 'Monica's last words. "It can hardly be without significance that Scotland is the only country, apart from Eire, Switzerland and Denmark, where teachers still think it necessary to flog their pupils."'

'To what?' said Mr Campbell, pencil poised over his crossword. Clue: *What are they when John has x times as many sweets as Jean*? 'That's a bit stupid, that is.'

He entered PROBLEM CHILDREN in his crossword and snorted.

'Flogging? The bitch doesn't know what flogging means.'

The bell rang. Harsh, crude, rude, dogmatic, domineering. Tea was gulped, cigarettes stubbed, pipes knocked out, crosswords abandoned till lunchtime, and the battle-scarred troopers marched out to rejoin their unit.

TWELVE

Mr Alfred went to see his aunt.

It was six weeks since he had given her any money. He swithered about sending her some by post. Then he thought it would be better if he went to see her.

'You're the fine one!' she said when she let him in.

'Your picture in the paper and you never come near folk to tell them what it was all about.'

'There was nothing to tell,' he said.

She scolded him.

'I thought you had more sense than to talk to reporters. Here, have a cup of tea.'

He sat down with his coat on and his old hat on his lap.

'I don't talk to them. One of them tried to talk to me. All I said was excuse me.'

'More fool you. You're lucky he didn't put in his paper, teacher apologises. But you must have been standing talking to them if they took your picture.'

He sat across from her and stirred his tea.

'No, It wasn't like that,' he said. 'You know, it's a very odd thing but–'

'Here, I haven't sugared it,' she said. 'Don't sit there and try to tell me they snapped your face behind your back.'

She pushed a poke of sugar across to him. He scrabbled the spoon in it. The sugar was low.

'They took it before I knew. You know, it's a very odd thing. You can stop a person printing a letter he stole from you, but you can't stop him taking a quick snap at you and printing your photograph.'

'You can't call your face your own these days,' she said. 'Do you want a biscuit? Or can I fry you something?'

'Any more trouble lately?' he was asking. 'No, thanks, no.'

'Nothing much,' she said. 'You're quite sure? It would be no bother. Except I had my purse snatched yesterday. I don't know how you stay alive on what you eat. Well, my handbag it was actually, but my purse was in it. Are you quite sure?'

'Yes, quite sure, thanks. You don't know who it was?'

'No, I've no idea. It was that quick. All I saw was the turnup of his jeans. I was coming through the Weavers Lane.'

'I've told you not to use the Weavers Lane.'

'It saves me a good minute's walk to Ballochmyle Road.'

'What happened?'

'I had my shopper and my handbag in one hand and somebody came up behind me and hit my wrist with a stick or something and I dropped them and he pushed me down and kicked me and grabbed my handbag and ran away. All I saw was the turnup of his jeans. Blue. Kind of tight. There was nothing I could do. He was out the lane and out of sight before I got to my feet. The funny thing was I found my handbag at the end of the lane but my purse was missing.'

He gave her more money than he had meant to.

'You shouldn't bother,' she said. 'The price of things these days. You need it yourself. I wish you'd buy yourself a new coat. And as for that hat. It's the midden it should be in.'

'I must get you a purse,' he said. 'You only ever had the one.'

'It was my mother's. It was a good one. They don't make them like that nowadays. Handstitched leather. It was a good one.'

'Yes, I know. I'll buy you a good one.'

'When would you buy a purse? The only shops you're ever in are beershops. I suppose you'll be off round them tonight as usual.'

He didn't deny it, and she let him go after he gave her his version of the Provan story. He kept saying at the doorstep he would get her a good purse like the one she had lost and she kept telling him not to bother.

His wandering took him to a district he hadn't visited for over a year. The pubs were all changed. More chromium and plastic, less mahogany and brass. But it was the new people in The Kivins, a bar he used to like, that spoiled his pub-crawl. He remembered it as a bright spot off the beaten track, frequented by characters he would have said Dickens rather than God created. He hardly knew the place, and he certainly didn't know the customers.

There used to be community-singing in the back-room, and many solos too, though singing of any kind was against the licensing laws. There was an Irish labourer sang 'Danny Boy', commonly known as the 'Londonderry Air', and even 'Sonny Boy', as well as 'The Rose of Tralee' and 'I love the dear silver that shines in your hair', which is the same song as 'Mother Machree', sung elsewhere by Count John McCormack. And every Saturday night a bookie's clerk sang 'I have heard the mavis singing', a fine song for a man with a good drink on him if he is a good tenor. The point of the song was that the voice of Bonny Mary of Argyll was sweeter than the song of the mavis, and a member of the audience said one night that the song was written by Rabbie Burns and that Bonny Mary of Argyll was Mary Campbell, the Ayrshire bard's Highland Mary.

His gloss aroused considerable dissension in the company and the argument flowed out of the back-room into the bar. Mr Alfred was appealed to as arbiter, his erudition being no doubt immediately recognised from his distinguished appearance and the fact that he wore a hat. He remembered the night well. He had, he regretted later, become rather didactic and after settling the controversy he had gone on to inform his fellow-drinkers that a similar mistake was often made about 'I dream of Jeannie with the light-brown hair'. Many people, he said, believed it was written by Burns when in fact it was the work of the American songwriter Stephen Foster who wrote about the old folks at home etc.

It was sober shame at his occupational habit of imparting information at the lowering of an elbow that inhibited him from going back to that haven of mirth and melody.

And now! Ah, now! No couthy customers chatted at the bar, no merry company sang the old songs through in the back-room. A television gabbled on a high shelf at the far end of the gantry and dazzled him with a watered-silk effect the moment he went in. Two trios of long-haired youths, apparently not on speaking terms, were plainly now the established patrons. The door of the back-room was open, and he saw a couple of bottle-blondes, haggard professionals, sitting there with middleaged men beside them. The waiters too were changed. Four hard-faced, wary-eyed silent men, moving like ex-boxers, served clumsily. They looked as if they didn't approve of drinking.

Having gone in, Mr Alfred was unwilling to turn round and go out again. He would have one drink there anyway. Half-way through his pint, staring straight in front of him, wishing he had gone to see Stella, he had a subliminal knowledge of quarrelsome voices rising, angry scuffling, and the approach of battle. These disturbances put an end to his meditation of Stella's bust and smile and he glanced round with disapproval. Two youths were fankled, legs kicking and heads butting, one of them with blood pouring from the tap of his nose. Four others, two on each side, tried to pull them apart, and there was a lot of bad language being used, another thing Mr Alfred didn't like.

The six youths came wrestling and lurching down the length of the bar, clearing all before them. Two of the ex-boxers dashed round to break it up and Mr Alfred stepped quickly out of their way, glass in hand. The youth who seemed to be the aggressor was wrenched away from his cowering foe but went on yelling threats and insults. He was a big fellow, and he strongly resisted the invulting arms of the grim barmen. He heaved himself free and launched a new attack. A joint effort by the bouncers brought him down, but in the tackle they shouldered Mr Alfred and brought him down too. He fell against a small table across from the bar and spilled beer all over his coat. When he got up he felt his ankle was hurting him. He hurried out as hastily as his newly-acquired claudication permitted, not waiting to hear what it was all about, nor caring.

He limped a hundred yards or so in great agitation before a familiar rain, tapping insolently on his bare head, told him he had lost his hat. He slowed down. Then he hobbled on. It was an old hat. Everybody laughed at it. He would rather spend money on a new one than go back for it. He kept going, head down against a wind, angry at the young ones who couldn't drink in peace.

By the time the pubs were closed the wind was worse. He stood in a bus-shelter and a rainy draught annoyed his legs. He felt his turnups getting soaked. He wondered why. Then he saw that the glass panels along the upper half and the metal panels along the lower half were all missing. He fretted as he waited. Five schoolboys across the street stopped a while and kicked at a litter-basket till it tumbled from its post. The wind took up their sport and played along the gutter with cigarette-packets, bus-tickets, orange-peel, pokes, cartons, and a vinegar-drenched newspaper that still remembered the fish and chips it had wrapped. A coca-cola bottle broke where it fell. The schoolboys slouched on to the next litter-basket.

'Oh dear me,' said Mr Alfred.

When the bus came he went upstairs for a smoke. There was a drunk man wouldn't pay his fare. The coloured conductor stood over him. Tall, patient, dignified, persistent. A good samaritan across the passage offered the money.

'No, no, oh no! That will not do,' said the coloured conductor. 'He must pay his own fare or go off.'

'Ach, go to hell,' said the drunk man, but quite pleasant about it.

He lolled unworried, a small man with a bristly chin and nothing on his head. Mr Alfred noticed the raindrops glisten on the balding scalp.

'Your fare please,' said the coloured conductor again.

'A belang here,' said the little drunk man. 'Mair than you do, mac. It's me pays your wages. Go and get stuffed.'

The bus weaved on between tall tenements.

'Pay your fare or I stop the bus,' said the coloured conductor.

'Ye kin stope it noo,' said the little drunk man. 'This is whaur A get aff.'

He swayed up as the bus slowed, palmed the coloured conductor out of his way, and slithered downstairs. Smiling. Victorious. Happy and glorious.

Mr Alfred caught the conductor's eye.

'You meet some types, don't you,' he said, anxious to show sympathy.

The conductor went downstairs without answering him.

Mr Alfred blinked drunkenly at the graffiti on the blackboard of the seat in front of him. The rexine had been torn off and on the bare wood someone had scrawled in loose capitals FUCK THE POPE. A different hand added underneath CELTIC 7–1. Most of the seats and large stretches of the rexine stripped away. The bus was as shabby as its route. Above the front-window SPITTING FORBIDDEN had been changed to SHITTING FORBIDDEN.

Mr Alfred sighed.

Three young men invaded the bus. They had shiny black jackets with white lettering on the back. ZEB ZAD ZOK I LOVE

THE ZINGERS. The last one on had the outline of a broadhipped female nude in yellow paint and LAW in brass studs. They were no sooner on than they rose to get off. The conductor stood in their way to collect their fares. The first shoved him aside, the second pushed past, and the third flashed a knife.

'There's wur fares,' he said. 'Ur ye wanting it?'

He rammed his knee in the conductor's testicles and went smartly on his way. The conductor straightened in time to catch him by the collar at the top of the stairs.

'Away ye big black cunt,' said the young man, kicking as he turned. 'Take yer hauns aff me or A'll do ye.'

He jerked free and did a wardance on the steps. The conductor kicked him on the thigh. He kicked back. The bus turned a corner. Rainbeads rolled down the streaming windows. White man and coloured, both fell. When they got up the passenger took another kick at the conductor. The conductor danced backwards and whipped off his ticket-machine. He swung it by the straps.

Mr Alfred jumped up to restrain him.

'Here! Don't! You'll kill him with that.'

He was frightened.

A buckle of the strap smacked him on the cheekbone and tore across the nose. The conductor's elbow thumped him on the eye in the course of a vicious parabola.

Mr Alfred clung to him.

'Let go, you,' said the coloured conductor.

Mr Alfred pulled him back. 'I'm only trying to help you,' he said. 'For your own good. You'd brain him if that thing landed.'

The passenger decamped. His mates were already off.

'Muck of the world,' said the coloured conductor. He was shaking. 'They won't pay. Every night they won't pay their fare. White bastards.'

'Compose yourself,' said Mr Alfred.

Turning to sit down again he saw a bus-inspector huddling in the back seat. He looked down on him. The bus-inspector looked up and shrugged.

'Well, what can you do with that kind?' he asked.

Mr Alfred had a black eye the next morning, a bruise on his cheek, and an abrased nose. But he wouldn't stay off work. He never did. When he turned up at school his colleagues were sure he had been in a drunken brawl. His awkward gait showed an injured ankle was bothering him.

'He's falling apart, that fellow,' said Mr Brown to Mr Campbell. 'I'll have to get rid of him. I'm going to have a quiet word with Briggs about him.'

THIRTEEN

Martha was sorry for Mr Alfred.

'Not that I know him. But every time I see him in the corridor, I mean. I was never in his class. Well, he never takes girls' classes. No, it's just when I see him about the school. I don't know. He looks so neglected.'

Graeme Roy laughed. He wasn't jealous. He couldn't see Mr Alfred as a rival.

'You want to mother him? He could be your father.'

'No, he couldn't.'

'Of course he could.'

'Of course he couldn't. In the first place my mother never met him. And even if she had I doubt if. I mean, she's not his kind.'

'I mean his age.'

'Who's talking about his age? All I said was I feel sorry for him. All that stinky stuff in the papers. The poor man always gets the low boys' classes.'

'You mean the boys' low classes.'

'No, I don't. I mean the low boys' classes.'

'I wouldn't say that. He taught me once.'

'He taught you? You never told me that. You been hiding your murky past from me?'

They liked to mention their past as if they had one and make little confessions about it that they never made to anyone else.

'In third year. Before they started the comprehensive.'

'Did you like him?'

'He was all right. A bit sarcastic maybe.'

'I can't stand sarcastic teachers.'

'I don't mean he was all that sarcastic. Just sometimes.'

'Tell me anybody that's sarcastic all the time.'

'Don't nag.'

'I'm not nagging. I was only asking a question. That's not nagging.'

'The way you do it it is. And it wasn't a question. It was an order. You said, tell me!'

'Who's nagging now?'

'Not me. It was you. I was only trying to tell you about Alfy.'

'Well, go on. Tell me.'

'He was quite amusing at times when I had him. But half the things he said were quotations. We didn't know. At least I didn't know. Not till later on. He could be very cutting. Then I found out it was Shakespeare or Pope or somebody. How were we to know? In third year. I ask you.'

'Casting his pearls before swine.'

He heard it as 'perils' and counted. Three was enough. He was in no danger of trying to improve her. It was she as she was detained him.

'Put it that way if you like. But what's the point of quoting Shakespeare when nobody knows you're quoting Shakespeare? That's teachers of course. Of course some of them say, as Shakespeare said, or in the words of Pope. But Alfy never. He was wasting his time showing off to us he knew his Shakespeare.'

'Maybe he wasn't showing off. Maybe it came natural to him.'

'Shakespeare come natural? You're joking of course.'

They were happy blethering and arguing, happiest then perhaps. Certainly happier than they were later when they expected to scale the heights or plumb the depths or learn the meaning of it all. But even then they had their troubles. When they gave up Ianello's they tried other cafes near and not so near the school. None suited. They were either too small or too big, too cheap or too dear, either a pokey wee ice-cream shop for juveniles or an adult coffee-lounge where men twice their age smoked cigars. They were beaten. Graeme offered her an answer. Instead of meeting for twenty minutes on the way home from school Monday to Friday, meet one night a week for two or three hours. A return to what they did before the ban fell. Avoid suspicion by keeping it strictly to just once a week and varying the night.

'It's not the same,' said Martha.

'We'd gain on it,' he said. 'Arithmetically.'

'It's not a question of arithmetic. I'd rather see you every day, even if it's only a few minutes.'

'But this way's no good. By the time we've said hello it's time to say goodbye.'

'Don't exaggerate,' she laughed at him.

'By the time we find a place where we can talk, I mean,' he said.

He was getting a bit sulky with her.

And he didn't mean talk though he thought he did. The ambitions of a young male growing in him. The withheld nearness of her unknown body was having its effect on his blood. A demon in his ear told him he would get nowhere talking to her in a cafe or at the bus-stop. A meeting at night would let him find the place and opportunity to go further. He could use the car again. And when he found the place he would find the time. The time to seduce her. Or seduce himself. The demon left it all very vague.

Yet his imagination remained chaste. He wanted to be longer with her, closer to her. That was all. To know more. He began to have a documentary interest in the privacies of her life. He was curious about her underwear. He wanted to know what lipstick and powder she used, what earlier loves she had and how much she knew about making love. He wondered when her periods were and how much pain she suffered then. He wanted to know if she slept alone or shared a bed with a sister. He wanted to see her half-undressed for bed. He hadn't got as far as thinking of her without her clothes on. But his hands longed to learn the precise mould and strength of her flanks, her thighs and breasts.

Past that point his uninformed thoughts faltered. What he could see kept them busy enough. The sheen of her blonde hair made him want to stroke it. But he couldn't do that in a public place. Her pale hand, small-palmed and long-fingered, seemed mysteriously different from his own. He wanted to take it and make it as familiar as the square fist that was a congenital part of himself. But he knew she would be annoyed if he held her hand in public. When she laughed, and she was much given to laughing, the good teeth behind her unkissed lips made him long to be taken behind them, to enter into her. But it was a yearning for a penetration beyond physical space. So with her complexion. She was so blonde her pure skin gave him the illusion of seeing a transparency more spiritual than epidermal. There too she tempted him to dreams of passing through an insubstantial curtain and dissolving himself within her. Her nylon knees, uncovered by a schoolgirl's skirt, whispered to his unlearned hand. For a time the height of his ambition was to fondle them. But he couldn't do that either in a public place. He was tired of seeing her in public places.

'I'm not keen on it,' she was saying. 'It would mean more deceit. I hate telling lies to my mum and dad. And once you start.'

'It would be better than this.'

'It's like saying a square meal once a week is better than a sandwich every day. I don't know that's true.'

'If you're going to be crude about it,' he huffed. 'Talking about food!'

They were trying yet another cafe for the first time. A pop hit from the juke box rocked the walls. They winced together.

'If music be the food of love,' said Martha.

He wasn't amused. He was in a bad mood.

'Oh, don't start quoting Shakespeare at me,' he said.

'You're as bad as big Alfy. Maybe you'd rather go out with him. Hold his hand and stroke his fevered brow if you feel all that sorry for him.'

'Don't be ridiculous, little boy,' she said.

'I'm taller than you,' he said.

But he won in the end. She gave in. They began to meet once a week, a different night every time. Since they were both fond of their parents they felt guilty.

FOURTEEN

Gerald went back to school in triumph. Once her grievance was off the front page Mrs Provan took it to her local councillor, who brought it before the education committee, whose members decided the suspension was invalid. The headmaster's writ didn't run in the Weavers Lane after four o'clock.

'It's the last time I'll—' said Mr Briggs.

'Why bother about the little bastards?' asked Mr Campbell.

'Let's face it,' said Mr Dale. 'You can't win.'

'Alfy mucked that one up,' said Mr Brown. 'He should never have—'.

'Not after hours,' said Mr Campbell. 'Once it's after four, well—'

'They can commit murder and mayhem,' said Mr Briggs.

'You don't get much thanks, do you?' said Miss Ancill.

'One minute after the bell, one inch across that gate, and as far as I'm concerned they can,' said Mr Briggs.

'I'd suspend him,' said Mr Dale. 'From the bloody rafters.'

'Surely any grownup has a right to stop boys fighting anywhere,' said Miss Ancill.

'The position is,' said Mr Kerr, 'you have the authority to stop fights only at the time and place when fights don't occur, during school hours inside the school. At the time and place where fights do occur, after four o'clock outside the school, you have no authority.'

'Sod them all,' said Mr Dale.

Mr Alfred sipped his tea in the staffroom, stuck in a corner silent by himself at morning-break. He felt the world was like a crowded bus speeding past the stop. It had left him behind. The daily frustrations of public transport analogised his fate. He didn't get on. Even if the bus did stop and some of the queue was allowed on board he was the one that was put off. He was always the extra passenger the conductor wouldn't take. He was without a home, wife or child, without father, mother, sister, brother or wellwisher. He hadn't even a car. He was unnecessary in the world, superfluous, supernumerary, not wanted. Nobody would miss him. He was an exile in his native land. Not that he had any love for his native land. He rated it as a cipher, of no value until a figure was put before it. But it had no figures. It existed only as terra incognita to the north of England. Hence formerly known simply as N.B. Note well. A footnote. Whereas England was where they spoke the language he taught, the language he once thought he knew. But he had been refused an immigrant's visa there many years ago when nine publishers rejected his thiry-two poems. They had condemned him to stay where he was and go on waiting at the bus-stop till a hearse came along. He had silence and exile, but no cunning.

He had long forgiven the uninterested publishers. Maybe they were right not to want his poems. After all, they were the only arbiters he respected. The praise of a friend, if friend he ever had, would prove nothing. And now he didn't know what to do. He was too old to earn a living anywhere else. He knew it was possible there was a vacancy for a scavenger in the cleansing-department. But he was probably past the age limit. There was no job open to a middleaged man that would let him live in the manner to which he was accustomed. Besides the expenses of rent, food, clothing and transport, which everyone had to meet, he had additional necessities to budget for. He was a heavy smoker. He was a hardened drinker. And sometimes he bought paperbacks and even a book in hard covers. These indulgences were not to be gained on a scavenger's wages.

He suffered an unwanted memory of the way Gerald ambled into the classroom that morning wearing new jeans and an old smirk. A spasm of undiluted hatred convulsed his guts and pained his sour face. His long lean body shuddered. He knew the emotion was unworthy of a cultured man like himself. But it was there. A glow of shame as well as hate warmed his forehead.

But Gerald and his friends were in high spirits. At the school dinner they chucked spuds across the room when the teacher on duty had his back to them. They skited peas on the floor at the server's feet when she passed with a loaded tray against her big bosom. They poured salt ad lib on the sweets of the diners across the table. They rattled their cutlery with a cha-cha, cha-cha-cha accompaniment. Smudge and Poggy importuned the perambulating teacher.

'Please sir he spat on ma dinner.'

'Please sir A never. He done it on mines first.'

'Please sir he's telling lies. It was him.'

Accuser and counteraccuser waited to see what the teacher would do. He looked down on one and then the other, turned neutrally away, and went on perambulating.

They tried him again next time round.

'Please sir he put salt on m'ice cream.'

'Please sir he pinched mines.'

'Please sir kin we have mair ice-cream?'

The teacher plodded silently on.

After four o'clock they went to Ianello's for a celebration. Gerald ordered three cokes.

'And three lucies,' he added.

When Enrico served him he pretended he hadn't any money, fumbled tediously in all his pockets. Enrico had to be patient. He had always to be patient with the boys from Collinsburn. Gerald put the money out at last in slow instalments of small change. He picked up the three loose cigarettes and handed them round. Fag in mouth, lifting their coke with a straw in the bottle, they all turned from the counter and surveyed the premises.

Gerald strolled to his favourite table, drawing his satellites round him. They were bigshots with a reservation in a posh restaurant sitting down to a drink before they called a waiter and ordered a meal. They talked loud and long. But they missed an audience.

'Hey, Nello!' Gerald shouted. 'Is there nae dames come here noo?'

Enrico served a little girl with an iced lolly and ignored him.

'Whaur's Martha Weipers these days?' Poggy bawled.

He scraped his foot on the floor like a restive stallion and lolled his tongue lasciviously.

'Ach, her!' said Smudge. 'I bet she's been screwed by yon toffee-nose.'

Enrico said nothing.

Gerald grinned.

Wilma and Jennifer came in, pushing each other on their way over the threshold. They giggled. They were chewing bubble-gum, and a pink hemisphere was protruded and retraced irregularly from their lips. They joined the boys. Gerald was pleased. He welcomed Wilma and Poggy took care of Jennifer. Smudge entertained them with song and story. He was the court jester.

Enrico watched them. They could have been worse. Apart from pocketing a couple of ashtrays, scratching their initials on the paintwork, and lifting a handful of tubular-packed sweets on their way out, they gave him no bother. Enrico saw them steal the sweets. But he knew it was his own fault for leaving the display-box so accessible. When they were crossing the door he called after them.

'Tough guys, eh? Fly men! Don't want you back here!'

Gerald stopped, turned round.

'I saw you,' said Enrico. 'Next time I call the police. I warn you.'

Gerald raised his right hand, the palm in, and jerked two fingers forked at Enrico. Repeated the gesture, grinning.

He had only a month to go before he left school.

FIFTEEN

Tired of living unloved unloving Mr Alfred fell in love. She was only a child, five feet one, seven stone two. But you can't measure the depth of a man's love by the height and weight of its object.

It happened when he was meditating hatred rather than love. For the first time in his life he was given a class of girls.

Three periods a week. Monday, Wednesday, Friday. The last forty minutes of morning school. He complained.

'Somebody's got to take them,' said Mr Brown.

'Why me?' said Mr Alfred. 'You've cut my free time.'

'I've cut everybody's free time,' said Mr Brown. 'There's a shortage of staff. Or didn't you know?'

'Girls!' said Mr Alfred. He was disgusted. A gloomy man glumly niggling. 'What am I supposed to do with them?'

'Poetry Monday,' said Mr Brown. 'Oral composition Wednesday. Debates, speech training, anything like that. Use the tape recorder. Spot of written work on Friday. Kind of diary of the week, say. Call it creative writing. Encourage them to say what they think. Self-expression. It's only three periods. You can waffle your way through.'

'Waffling's more your line,' said Mr Alfred. 'Suppose they have nothing to express?'

'Self-expression, I like that,' said the eavesdropping Mr Dale. 'Makes it sound good, eh? Dumb weans. Self-expression my arse.'

'I'm paying you a compliment,' said Mr Brown. 'These are first year girls. I wouldn't give them to a man at all if I could help it. They can be such little bitches. I certainly can't give them to any of the younger men. I'm relying on you to keep them in order. Maybe even teach them something. A man of your experience and may I say sobriety.'

'I think your last word's a bit–' said Mr Alfred.

His head was high, his voice was cold. He saw an innuendo about his private life. He thought his aposiopesis more dignified than any word.

'I mean in class,' said Mr Brown. 'You have what the Romans called gravitas. There's no danger of you joking with them. I've always found it a mistake to make a joke with a class of girls. You lose them for good. It's different with boys. You can make a joke with them and then all right–joke over! That's it. But girls want to keep it up. They won't stop giggling. The young men coming in now, flippant types, they're no use with girls' classes. But you have that special air about you. Like one of Shakespeare's grave and reverend signiors.'

'Butter,' Mr Dale chanted.

'Othello,' said Mr Alfred.

Mr Brown was quite sincere. He was sure Mr Alfred was so humourless the girls would see no use trying to lead him on. There was plainly no fun to be had from him. He was such a sourpuss they would never think he was smashing or fab or terrific or out of this world or whatever their current word was for any male who excited their silly little minds. They would regard him as a dead loss, a square, a nutter, an oldie. They would settle down and perhaps do some work. If his guess was wrong he had nothing to lose. If a first year class of dim wenches were too slippery for Mr Alfred to control he could tell the headmaster the man had trouble with girls as well as boys. Then he could renew his plea to have him shifted.

The human need to find a silver lining through the dark clouds shining made Mr Alfred look for a ray of light on the Stygian session ahead of him. He tightened his jaws till his decadent molars ached the first morning he stood at his desk and watched this strange new class flood into his room. They were all agiggle, untidy and sweating after forty minutes in the gym, waddling, mincing, slouching, shuffling, hen-toed, splay-footed, unkempt, unclean, blacknailed, piano-legged, pin-legged, long and short, round and square, fat and thin, bananas and pears, big-breasted and flat-chested, chimps and apes, weeds and flowers, a dazzling tide of miscellaneous mesdemoiselles, twelve to thirteen years of age. Some wore nylons, some wore socks, some wore white hose to the knees, some had long hair, some had short, some had their hair styled, some wore it as it grew, some had washed their face that morning, some it seemed hadn't ever.

The ray he found was Rose Weipers. She sat down quietly on the front seat beside Senga Provan. They were conspicuously chums. But Gerald was gone. It was a new session. And Mr Alfred never believed in visiting the sins of the brother on the sister, far less on the sister's friend. When he was a political-minded young man he disliked the totalitarian countries where they proved guilt by association. He would take Senga as he found her, a person in her own right. He found her rather unattractive. Her scared strabismic face, her freckles and her ginger hair somehow embarrassed him. He avoided looking at her. But Rose was different. She was clean and tidy. She looked human, even intelligent. Before the week was out he was thinking she looked pretty as well.

He flicked through the progress-cards to find her IQ. It wasn't very high, just comfortably over the hundred. Senga's was higher. That irked him a little. He had prepared the comment that her very name showed she was backward. The rest, like the horses in the same race as Eclipse, were nowhere. He saw he had been given a giggle of the less academic girls just as last session he had been given a huddle of the less academic boys.

His only interest was Rose. He had a teacher's snobbery about IQs, a teacher's predilection for a welldressed child, a male weakness for a pretty face. When Rose came to him as a graceful trinity of good intelligence, good clothes and good looks, he had no choice. He made her his routine messenger. Whenever he had to pass on a circular from Mr Briggs it was always Rose Weipers he sent next door with the 'please initial' document.

It didn't take him long to make her an errand-girl at lunchtime too. He sent her out for a morning-paper, pretending he hadn't time to get one on his way in. In fact he never bothered much about seeing a morning-paper. But it gave him an excuse to have her come back to him when the class was gone. Then he stopped going to the school-dinners. He sent Rose to the local shops for rolls and cheese, rolls and gammon, a couple of hot mutton pies, anything he could take with a cup of tea in the staffroom. He didn't care what. He was never interested in food.

At first it was only when he had her in his class at the end of morning-school that he sent her on an errand. But within the month she was coming along uninvited on other days to ask if there was anything he wanted. He always thought of something, because when she came back it meant he had her alone for a few minutes.

Halfway through the term they had got into the habit of meeting every day at lunchtime. He would wait in his classroom. When she came to him he didn't touch her. He told the critic at the back of his mind he wasn't getting the girl to come to his empty room so that he could cuddle her. It was her simple presence, with no one watching, gave him pleasure. Just to be alone with her. That's what he thought.

Coming back after her first voluntary shopping for him she knocked some test-papers off his desk. She was parking a poke with two rolls and gammon and counting out his change. The papers glided under the poke and slipped to the floor.

'That's a good start,' she said.

She picked up the papers, tutting at herself but not flustered. He noticed the way she stooped, a girl's way, bending the knees to keep her thighs from being exposed, not straddled and straightlegged like a boy. There was a certain elegant modesty about the movement that pleased him. And he loved the way she said 'start'. As if they were beginning a new life together. He believed they were.

She had a talent for making conversation. She would talk to him the way she would talk to a friend her own age. But not always. She puzzled him. She was as unpredictable as the grown women he had tried to love when he was young. One day she was chatty, the next day she hadn't a word to say for herself. It was her confiding moods made him fall in love, as when she told him about her aunt.

'I cried myself to sleep last night,' she said, alone with him at his desk.

'Oh dear,' he said. 'What happened?'

He bent to listen. He forgot he had said he would never touch her. He was only trying to show sympathy. He put an arm round her shoulder as he inclined an ear. She moved in close, telling him.

Her Aunt Beth had been staying with them for three months and left yesterday to go to Corby and get married.

'I'll miss her,' said Rose. 'She was so good to me. I was awful fond of her.'

He was no Alfred Lord Tennyson to object to her 'awful'. He squeezed her shoulder.

'But you'll see her again,' he said. 'It's not the end of the world.'

His hand wandered down her shoulder and stroked her arm.

He was sure she had an affectionate nature. Her talk was always about people she was fond of.

'My dad's been promising for weeks to take me to *The Sound of Music*,' she said. 'We were to go last night. But I didn't get.'

'You'll learn that's how life is,' he said, instructing her in banalities by occupational habit. 'You look forward to something and then it doesn't come off. I hope you weren't too disappointed.'

'Oh, no,' she said. 'I was more concerned about my dad. He wasn't well. That's why. He was sent home from his work. He's in bed. My mum got the doctor in.'

He liked the solemn way she said 'concerned'. He liked the word itself since it came from her young lips. He thought the sick man was lucky to have Rose concerned about him.

She told him of Martha's high marks in exams. She was proud of her big sister.

'Martha's clever,' she said. 'Not like me.'

He didn't know Martha, didn't want to. It was enough knowing Rose. He would have preferred her to be without a family, existing only for him. To think of her having a sister diminished her uniqueness.

Her innocent conversation made him think she liked him. He was a happy man. He teased her sometimes.

'That's a fine face you've got today! What's the matter with you? You look fed up.'

'I'm fed up,' she said, fed up. She gave him his poke and his change. 'This weather. Put years on an elephant, so it would.'

Nonstop rain and low graphite skies for a fortnight. A damp dismal world they lived in.

'Season of mists,' he said.

Rose sniffed, not hearing or not caring.

'I've got a cold,' she said.

'You stay in your bed tomorrow,' he said.

It gave him a warm feeling of intimacy to mention bed to her, to think of her there.

'Dear me, look at your hair!' he cried. 'It doesn't know which way it's going.'

Emolliated with affection he stroked her hair from crown to nape, smoothed it back from her ear. Finger-tip on an auricle. So tender.

'Can't do a thing with it,' she said. 'Washed it last night.'

She slanted her head away. He felt his hand rejected.

Then she made him jealous. He was waiting at his classroom door for her return from the shops. The sight of her coming along always made him love her. She looked so young, so remoted from the world's slow stain, so trim and brave, so lonely and devoted, coming back to him and him alone, he was soothed to tenderness, his vanity gratified. She always seemed so much smaller outside the classroom, more of a child, he felt quite paternal.

He saw her meet the gym-teacher in the corridor. Cantering along, lightfooted in plimsolls, the gym-teacher grabbed her by the arm, birled her. Mr Simmons. A eupeptic, bigchested, broadshouldered young man.

'Hiya, Rose!' he greeted her.

He plunged his hand into her thick brown hair and ruffled it. Rose stopped, head down, accommodating the exploring hand, laughed. Mr Simmons weaved, boxing at her, clipped her lightly on the chin.

'I'll bang you,' said Rose.

She raised a miniature fist. She was pink and delighted.

Mr Simmons danced round her on his toes. Rose shaped up to him, leading with her right but handicapped by holding in it the poke with Mr Alfred's lunch. They made a palaestra of the deserted corridor. Still sparring even as they parted they both seemed pleased with the brief encounter.

'You don't get Mr Simmons for PT, do you?' said Mr Alfred dourly. He took the poke and change. He had a grudge against her for being so pretty that another man liked her. 'How does he know you?'

'Everybody knows me,' said Rose.

'Indeed?' he said, still sulky.

'I get him sometimes,' Rose explained. 'He takes the netball team for practice after four when Miss Avis can't stay.'

'But you're not in the netball team,' he challenged her. Very suspicious he was. 'At your age.'

'Not the school team, that's sixth year,' she said. She clicked her tongue at his absurd quizzing. 'The class team I mean, for the class league.'

He didn't know anything about class teams and a class league. She was helpless at his huff and left at once. So he got no conversation that day. It troubled him. He had been afraid he was in love. Now he was sure. Given the choice, he would rather have an hour with Rose than a night with Stella.

He couldn't stop thinking of Mr Simmons wrestling with Rose in the corridor. It was so natural, so harmless. Nobody could say there was anything improper in it. Rose had taken it laughing. Obviously she liked Mr Simmons. Her threat to bang him was an example of the free and easy relations between a modern pupil and a modern teacher. She would never have said it to him. But then he could never have done what Mr Simmons did. He wished he could.

He knew the trouble lay in his own bad mind. He wanted to fondle Rose. But his bad mind inhibited him. He was afraid if anyone saw him he would get the name of a lecherous old man. Even if nobody saw him Rose might be offended or frightened. She might know what evil creatures men could be. But she could let Simmons ruffle her hair and wrestle with her because she trusted Simmons. Of course Simmons was a married man with two little girls. Simmons was a man used to showing affection. Simmons had the right touch.

His bad mind kept annoying him. There was no use saying he could no more assault Rose than fly in the air, it would be against the gravity of his nature. He could imagine many things he would never do. He could imagine himself committing suicide though he knew he never would. He had come near it the day he knew his poems would never be published, and given up the idea for good. It wasn't in his nature. He could imagine himself attacking Rose to feel her breasts and lift her skirt. He knew he never would. But he knew such things were done by men his age to girls her age. His fear was that by some misconstrued telepathy Rose might suppose he intended the enormities he sadly knew were practised if he tried to play with her the way Simmons had done.

Whenever he read in the papers the story of a schoolgirl raped and murdered he was horrified at what a man could do. But it wasn't incomprehensible, it wasn't unthinkable. He could think it easily enough. He could imagine the damnable deed in all its details. But he was certain he could never do it himself. Any more than he could stick a knife into somebody, though he could imagine doing it. An indecent assault on Rose was one of the sins he knew he could never commit. Yet he longed to kiss her goodnight, to see her into bed. He longed to say he loved her. But never to love her by force. It was the lack of affection in rape that shocked him.

He was interested when he saw a story in the papers about a man of sixty marrying a girl of twenty. He worked out the difference between his own age and Rose's. It was less than that. So marrying her, however improbable, wasn't impossible. There were precedents. But at the same time as he thought of marrying Rose in a daydream future he kept thinking of her as his daughter in the waking life of his present.

The sodden autumn drained into a freezing winter. She came back carrying the quotidian poke, her hands blue with cold.

He took one. He was upset to feel it so chilled on his errand.

'Che gelida manina,' he said.

She looked up and said nothing. Puzzled. Wondering what he said.

He put the poke aside and chafed her hands. She let him do it without a word for or against, watching the operation with silent catatropia, and he was content.

After that he got into the habit of taking her hands when they were alone. He would pretend they looked cold and rub them. Then he stopped pretending. He held out his hand for hers while she was talking to him. The first time, she didn't understand what he meant. When he put his hand out she thought he was pointing to something on the floor at her feet and she looked down for something to be picked up. But the second time she saw what he wanted and gave him her hands with a kind of motherly patience. It became a daily ritual, this holding of hands as they chatted alone at lunchtime, and he gave her half-a-crown every Friday. He called it her pocket-money.

Christmas was coming. He thought he would give her a money-present in recognition of the season and her services. He was all set for a tender donation when she came back with his rolls and beat him to the love-scene he planned.

'I've got a wee present for you,' she said.

She smiled up at him with a child's excitement at the time of gifts and peace on earth, the holy tide of Christmas, brimming over with good-will.

She gave him a box of ten small cigars. Holly and a robin and From and To on the cardboard wrapping.

'They'll be a change for you,' she said. 'From those cigarettes you're aye smoking. I buy these for my dad at Christmas.'

He felt numbered among her clan.

'You shouldn't have done that,' he said.

He blushed as he took the nuzzer. Rose smiled.

'I was going to give you something,' he said. 'But I didn't know what to get you. You buy yourself something.'

He slipped a pound note into her drooping hand. It was a new one kept specially for her.

Rose palmed the note with a discretion equal to his. She looked up at him brighteyed and happy but didn't say thanks.

'If you were an orphan I'd adopt you,' he blurted.

He wanted to kiss her. But he was so tall he couldn't get his mouth to hers without an awkward swoop that would spoil the spontaneity of the action, and she didn't hold her face up to help him. He settled for squeezing her hand as it closed on the money.

When she went away he found he was tumescent. He argued with the man inside that it was only a desire to give her all the love he had. Not a stupid lust, but an erotic urge to an impossible act of gratitude.

He was drunk that night. He always got drunk in the euphoria of starting a holiday from school. Recognising the face in the mirror of a public-house gents he made a face at it, questioned it.

'Well, wotta ya gotta say for yourself, eh?' he asked, swaying to the glass. 'Sennimennal old fool. Wanting to kiss Rose. Rose upon the rood of time. Red Rose, proud Rose, sad Rose of all my days. Rose of the world, Rose of Peace. Far off, most secret and inviolate Rose. You want to frighten her? Stick your ugly mug into her lovely face and what would she get? A child's sense of smell. The reek of tobacco and the smell of whisky. A fine Christmas that for Rose. A merry kiss-miss. Be your age, mac!'

He had never been at parties when he was a boy. He had never played at kissing-games. He had only heard of them. He thought a kiss was too serious for games. It wouldn't be right to kiss Rose. He loved her too much to snatch an old man's peck at her. He should leave her to get her first kiss from someone she loved when she was older.

SIXTEEN

Mrs Provan got Gerald a job beside her in the biscuit factory. She was never backward in asking. She kept on at the man in charge of deliveries till he started Gerald as a vanboy. There was no future in it, but it was a job. She would find him something better in due course. Gerald liked it. The work wasn't hard and the money was good. It was a carefree life, sitting in the van beside the driver, whistling and singing. He learnt his way round his native city, stopping here and there, kidding and kissing the shopgirls and getting known as Gerry. He was growing up, a handsome lad, and at the weekend he had money in his pocket. His mother let him keep most of his pay.

'He's not going to have the hard life I had,' she said to her foreman. 'I got on for years without a penny from him. I can still manage, please God. It'll do him good to have money to spend. He'll learn to look after himself.'

But she looked after him just the same as before, and Gerald's money went without either of them knowing exactly where. He never bought a suit or a pair of shoes, never a shirt or a tie, and when he had to get a haircut he asked his mother for the money. When he started shaving she bought his razorblades and shavingsoap until she got him an electric razor for his birthday. At his summer holidays he expected a bonus from her. He always got it.

He spent most of his nights in Ianello's, but time was all he spent. He never paid for his soft drinks or ices or sweets or cigarettes. He told Enrico he would see him later. He was a big, stronglooking boy, intimidating, largehanded, bold-eyed, insolent, armed. He had a knife he let people get a glimpse of when it suited him. Not the one Mr Alfred had seen. A new one, a bigger one. He challenged opposition with the glint of it to see what would happen. Nothing happened. He never used his knife. He got his own way with the show of it. Poggy and Smudge were what he called his handers. They admired him. Enrico suffered him for the sake of peace and quiet.

It was worse for Enrico when Jennifer and Wilma came in. It led to competition. The young males kept chancing their arm to prove who was the hard man. They peacocked, disputatious. The young hens egged them on, squawking and screeching. In the upshot Gerald stayed boss of the cafe. He had this knife. Enrico sighed, and settled for peace, though there wasn't much quiet with it. The jukebox he had hoped would bring in a jolly company of regular guys and dolls was monopolised by a dissident sect that kept other communicants away.

Gerald's mother never asked him where he went at night but she was always worrying about his future.

'You learn to drive that van, son,' she said. 'Never mind what your pals do. If you can drive you'll always find a job.'

'What do you think I'm doing?' said Gerald. 'I aim to get a car of my own. You've got to have a car nowadays to be anybody.'

He loved the smell of petrol and oil, the motorodour of a garage, the sights of jacks and pumps and wrenches and spanners, he loved lolling in the van and grinning at the panic-stricken pedestrians who had to scamper back or scurry across when the van came breezing through at the changing of the lights.

He bought magazines about motorcycles and cars and kept them stacked under his bed. He read them through over and over again, hoarding an enormous specialist knowledge. He could identify any vehicle at a hundred yards, make, model and year. But when he saw the price of a good secondhand car he lowered his sights to getting a motorbike first. The visceral image of the speed he could get on a motorbike excited him. It was like the way Jennifer and Wilma excited him when they leaned back crosslegged in Ianello's wearing a miniskirt. He felt an urge to get on and on. Faster and faster. Onwards and ever upwards. He was growing up.

'They won't keep you on once you're older,' his mother warned him. 'Once a vanboy wants a man's wage they just sack him and get another boy. There's never any shortage of boys.'

'I wonder why that is,' said Gerald.

He winked at Senga behind his mother's back. Senga gave him a crosseyed snub. She was against him. She was loyal to Rose Weipers. She loved Rose Weipers. And she knew Mr Alfred was always getting Rose to go errands for him. She didn't mind. There was no envy in her. She knew Rose had the prettier face. She was ready to like any teacher who liked Rose. But Gerald and her mother still kept on about Mr Alfred. They told her to stand up to him. She never found any occasion to, and kept her opinion to herself. Once in a month or so she had her childhood dream again, that she was sitting on her father's knee, or some man's knee. She couldn't remember the face. Before he kissed her she wakened up. The only person she ever told was Rose.

Gerald wasn't bothered about her. She was only his sister. He had a lot more on his mind than her silences. In the yard where the fleet of factory-vehicles was parked he was learning starting and stopping, gear-changing, reversing and three-point turns. Hill-starting and stopping he learnt on Tordoch Brae on Saturday afternoons by plenary indulgence of the driver at the end of the week's deliveries. He found it difficult at first. But he was interested, he concentrated, determined to learn. He was full of himself and nobody ever said he wasn't intelligent. He was never nervous sitting in charge of a powerful, throbbing vehicle. He knew it was under his control. He was the lord of an engine that slavishly obeyed the touch of his hand and foot. He was the triumph of mind over metal. But apart from the lessons on hill-starting the driver wouldn't let him take over outside the factory.

His mother was passing across the yard once when she saw him getting a lesson. A smile thawed her frozen face. To see him sitting up there in the cabin driving the van pleased her.

'You know,' she said to her foreman, 'it's an awful pity his teachers took a spite at him. They taught him nothing. Gerald could have been an engineer if he'd got the education.'

She was a patient woman, crafty, for ever planning ahead. Well in advance of the time when Gerald would be too old to stay on as a vanboy she was on to the maintenance men in the firm's garage. She deaved them how good her Gerald was, what a smart boy, quick to learn, a willing worker. She got him started as an apprentice motor-mechanic. Poggy and Smudge went into the same line. Poggy found a job in a bus-company's garage and Smudge scraped a place in a local petrol and repair station. They were all happy. It kept them sharing a way of life.

In the evenings when it was boring sitting any longer in Ianello's talking shop, they swaggered out for diversion. They finished up on the prowl after midnight. They kicked over the wire litter-bins on the arc-lamp standards, lifted the empty milk-bottles outside a sleeping house and smashed them on the road. They chucked stones at the crossing-beacons. When they passed a bus-shelter with any panes still unbroken they broke them.

Tired mooching around like that, Gerald was the first to get a bike. Always at his heels, Poggy and Smudge got one as well. Gerald's was on monthly payments. It was new. Poggy and Smudge got second-hand ones cheap. The three of them overworked their bikes. Parts had to be replaced. But they couldn't go on buying them. It cost too much. There wasn't much they could lift where they worked that was any use to them. So at one and two in the morning they raided any motor-bikes parked in the street. Sometimes they stripped a bike for the fun of it. When they had more spares than they needed Smudge sold the surplus to any motor-cyclist who used his repair-shop and asked no questions about a bargain.

Smudge was the first to steal a bike. His own was past it. After all, it was in its second childhood when he bought it. He swopped the numberplates and ditched his own in the quarry behind the brickwork. They moved on to cars. Many a man in the housing-schemes had a car but no garage. He had to leave his car in the street all night. Gerald took Poggy and Smudge with him ambling round side-streets after midnight looking for vulnerable vehicles. They had a good collection of car-keys. They stripped a car of its radio, its battery, raided the boot. Anything left in the back seat they lifted.

'Bugger doesn't deserve to get keeping it,' Smudge used to say when he fished out a briefcase, an A.A. handbook, a mascot, a paperback or magazine. Any trifle at all, he took it.

They had a good night in a quiet crescent of semi-detached villas far from their own territory. There were a dozen cars parked along it. They smashed the windows, forced open any door they couldn't unlock, and stole the car-seats and travelling-rugs. They tossed the car-seats into somebody's front-garden well away from where they got them. Poggy and Smudge shared the travelling-rugs between them.

Gerald didn't want one. He never took home anything that was stolen.

It was nearly two in the morning when he got home from that raid. He had been getting later and later, but this was the worst ever. His mother was angry.

'Where have you been till this time?' she shouted.

'You've had me worried stiff!'

'Ach, shut your face, you old nag,' said Gerald.

He was tired, and that made him a bit short with her. He stared hard at the bare table.

'What've you got?' he asked. 'You don't mean to say there's nothing ready for me.'

Mrs Provan was distressed. She couldn't think what to say for a moment.

'I can fry you a sausage and an egg if you like,' she said humbly.

'That'll do fine,' said Gerald agreeably. He never kept up a bad mood.

Senga, conscripted to sit up with her anxious mother, made a face unseen and slipped off silent and unnoticed to bed.

SEVENTEEN

Graeme Roy went to the university. He was excited but confident, a young hawk eager to swoop on a new field. Martha stayed on at school for another year to add to her leaving-certificate subjects. She liked French and German. She thought she would get a cosmopolitan job with a good degree in modern languages. They looked forward to being students together. He saw himself as the trail-blazer, preparing the way for his soul-mate. With a year's experience in hand he would be able to guide and advise her, take her round the scattered buildings of the university, lead her to the French and German departments and the women's union, tell her what clubs and societies she ought to join.

But he had no one to show him around. He enrolled in engineering and missed lectures in the opening weeks because he didn't know where they were being given. When he settled to the work of his classes he discovered he was a country yokel in a mob of city slickers, a flounder in a shoal of smart students. He wanted to be a technocrat. That was how he saw it, that was how he said it. But he wasn't up to it. He had poor results in the first term exams at Christmas, the Christmas Mr Alfred and Rose Weipers were holding hands. When it came to summer and the degree exams he was in a panic. He lost the place in all his subjects. He couldn't decide which one to worry about most. He worried about them all and couldn't concentrate on one in particular. When the results went up on the board he saw he had failed in them all.

It wasn't Martha's fault. Much as she liked to be with him she wouldn't meet him oftener than once a week. She encouraged him to study. She wanted to be proud of being his girlfriend. She wanted to find him established at the university when she arrived there. She wanted him to be a student who had passed all his first year exams without any bother and who would pass all his exams the same way every year until he graduated with an honours B.SC. degree in Engineering.

His total failure made her miserable. She wept in the loneliness of her bed. He was sullen after he told her he had nothing to tell her. He blamed the system. He said there had always to be so much percent of a plough, and he had fallen below an arbitrary line. He was sure he hadn't done all that badly, he surely deserved a pass in at least one of the subjects. She blamed his father for persuading him to take a degree in engineering. But only to herself. She never came out with it to him. And amid her sorrow she wasn't surprised at his failure. She had felt all along he had picked the wrong course.

His old teachers, always informed of university results, were as little surprised as Martha.

'I don't know what comes over these fellows,' said Mr Kerr. 'I advised him to take an Arts degree.'

'He should have gone in for English Honours,' said Mr Brown. 'He had a talent for English. He wrote a very good poem for last year's magazine.'

'An engineering degree is just about the hardest degree there is,' said Mr Campbell. 'There's a heavy plough every year. And Graeme Roy and engineering maths, well, I ask you! He's a nice lad all right but no head for maths. I saw that when I had him in my last class. What makes them do it?'

'They put a glamour round it,' said Mr Brown. 'An Arts degree is too common for them, thank you.'

'That's true,' said Mr Dale. 'They get this science bug. They want to be back-room boys.'

'They think the ambition proves the capacity,' said Mr Campbell.

'His whole bent was for languages,' said Mr Kerr.

'He showed me a translation he had made of a poem by Rimbaud, "le Formeur du Val". I'd never ask a schoolboy to translate Rimbaud.'

'But wasn't Rimbaud only a schoolboy when he wrote it?' said Mr Dale.

'Yes, I know,' said Mr Kerr. 'But he was Rimbaud. I would never take Rimbaud's poems with any class here. But Roy had been reading French poetry on his own, God bless him. He wanted my opinion of his translation. I said it was quite good. So it was.'

'That poem he wrote for me,' said Mr Brown.

'For the magazine I mean. It was a case of Dylan Thomas out of Swinburne. Very good as I said. But I couldn't print it.'

'Why not?' Mr Alfred enquired sharply from his corner.

Anything concerning poetry concerned him. He had never seen the poem Mr Brown was talking about nor had he ever heard before of the translation from Rimbaud. He was annoyed. He thought he should have been consulted.

'Well, in a school magazine!' said Mr Brown.

'There are limits, you know. He was only a boy of seventeen at the time. He shouldn't have been thinking the way he was, not at his age. Kind of sexy it was.'

'I see,' said Mr Alfred. 'And at what age if not seventeen should he be thinking of sex? Folk like you would have us either too young or too old.'

'You mean you still—' Mr Brown began.

'A man's never too old,' Mr Dale tactfully interrupted. 'Look at that old bloke of sixtyfour in the papers yesterday married a wench of nineteen. His grand-daughter's chum.'

Mr Alfred had seen it but didn't like to mention it.

'That's all very well,' said Mr Brown. 'But there was one bit I remember. Something about, I dream in these satyric moods of nymphs' wan thighs in summer woods. I could never have printed that. What would old Briggs have said? Not to mention the parents.'

'Or our beloved Monica the All-Seeing,' said Mr Dale.

'I had him some years back,' said Mr Alfred. 'He seemed quite intelligent, but I should never have thought there was a poet in him.'

He sat back and said no more. He was no longer interested in the conversation. It had made him think of Rose Weipers. Everything made him think of Rose Weipers. He had never seen her thighs. He tried to imagine them. He couldn't. She was always sedate, sat down like a lady, knees and feet together. Even in the playground, any time he passed and took a quick look, she managed to jump the rope in her turn without the swirling skirt and swift show of thigh that other girls flaunted. She never showed off. He had seen without interest the legs and underwear of other girls as they lolled in his room, but Rose never showed an inch above the hemline. She was a modest girl. His autumnal longing to kiss a child goodnight and tuck her into bed moved through him again. He had a passionless wish, a neutral and almost clinical curiosity, to see Rose as she was, from head to toe, whole and entire.

'He had an unusual Sprachgefühl,' said an assistant German teacher. 'I told him he ought to—'

'He had a good French accent,' said an assistant French teacher. 'Before he left I said to him—'

'I warned him,' said Mr Campbell. 'I said to him you might be good at English but as far as maths are concerned you're—'

'I advised him,' said Mr Brown. 'What you should do I said is–'

'They get this craze about science,' said Mr Kerr. 'They want to be with it. But where's the culture in all these technical subjects?'

The bell rang. Nobody answered.

They went to their classes. They dropped Graeme Roy. But I can't. Not yet, anyway.

Having failed to satisfy the examiners he wanted to satisfy Martha. There at least he would prove he wasn't an impotent failure. He tried to arouse her. She wasn't aroused. She was only offended. The nearer he tried to get the further away she moved. When he sulked and withdrew she warmed to bring him back. Her temperature seemed to vary inversely with his.

In the summer vacation he took her out one day in his car. The parents had guessed they were meeting again but didn't want to make a new fuss about an old issue. They were prepared to tolerate though not to encourage an affair which had persisted in spite of them. They were willing to concede the young couple were getting old enough to know their own mind. It might be a case of true love after all.

They went to Helensburgh and up the Garelochhead, then followed Loch Long north to Arrochar and lunch. They were lucky in the weather. The sky was an unbroken blue and the cloudless windless heat made them feel they had wandered into a day from the legendary summers of the past. On a lonely stretch they saw the opposite bank reflected in the motionless water of the mirroring loch. It was an inverted world of tall timeless trees and unpeopled hills. Nothing moved anywhere. They got out.

'Listen!' she cried suddenly.

He smiled, she was so happy.

Obeying her he listened. He clasped her hand and looked up at the immense sky because she was looking there. A birdsong rose higher and higher and faded to heavenly silence. But he could see nothing.

'The lark in the clear air,' he said.

They sat in the car a little while before going on. He wanted to find release in her, to lean on her, to be comforted and encouraged. Not this time as the times he offended her, not the male determined to conquer his woman by force, but the defeated manchild turning to the female for motherly solace. She gave him none. Her breast wasn't going to be his pillow. Her retreat made him impatient. He pulled her tight against him and kissed her harder than he had ever kissed her before. And longer. She was so close, his alert body was aware of her heartbeat. It was going at a terrific rate. He thought he had only to keep at her a moment more and she would give in. But the racing throb of that necessary engine frightened him. So fast her heart was going it seemed it could only end in a crashing stop. Let it beat for ever, he prayed, let me not disturb it further. There was plenty of time. He slackened his grip. A wave of tenderness drowned him. He let her sit away from him.

She turned suddenly and kissed him gently on the cheek. Her hand was stroking the back of his neck. He felt it was a medal awarded for devotion to duty in face of the enemy.

They went from Arrochar to Tarbet. She saw the Cobbler on her left hand. It was all new to her. She was dumb with delight. Her eyes were excited, but he knew it was only by the countryside in fine summer weather, not by anything he had done to her. He grudged her taking pleasure in nature and not in him. But he put a face on it and drove chatting up Loch Lomond to Ardlui, on to Crianlarich and through Glen Dochart. He turned south into Glen Ogle and took her home by Callander, Loch Vennacher and Aberfoyle. She had never seen so much of the country outside her city. She was exhausted at the end of the long day, dazed with strange sights. The bens and glens and lochs, the sheep and highland cattle, the remote cottage and the blue sky over all, the lonely miles where there were no streets and no shops and no tenements or housing-schemes, still lingered in her town-reared brain. When she closed her eyes that night in bed alone she saw them again. Without him she would never have seen them at all. She told him so. He was pleased to have pleased her, even if it wasn't the way he had meant. It was another knot in the string that tied them.

EIGHTEEN

Granny Lyons used Ianello's cafe nearly every day. She bought her cigarettes there. She didn't smoke a lot, but she was never without a packet. Once in a while, if Mr Alfred hadn't come when she expected him and she was short of money, Enrico let her have a packet on tick. She was fond of sweets too, and got them in the same shop. Usually it was only a half-pound of liquorice-all-sorts, a mixture she particularly liked, almost to the point of addiction. Whenever she tried to do without them for more than a week Enrico slipped her a box with her cigarettes. Then he would turn away from her, his elbow on the counter, and look up and down and all along his shelves as if he was surveying his stock and hadn't given her anything, didn't even know she was there.

They were friends. They shared the sorrow of having blundered into Tordoch when they had set sail for a different port altogether. They were bewildered and frustrated, the way Columbus was when he tripped over the West Indies instead of making landfall in Asia. They couldn't understand what had gone wrong with their navigation. Granny Lyons saw no escape. She knew it was a life-sentence, at her age. Enrico was younger and so more optimistic. He said he would move to a better area soon and get a good-going shop.

She liked to hear him talk about his plans. His accent charmed her. His voice was more lively and his tone more varied than anything the natives could manage with their flat utterance of half-swallowed syllables. She was fascinated by the energetic movement of his lips and the expressive assistance of his hands and shoulders. She preferred the vigorous activity of his mouth under the drooping moustache to the slack-jawed speech of his customers who mumbled at him with their hands in their pockets.

His vocabulary too amused her. He knew all the dialect words and the local slang. He came out with the standard obscenities as fluently as anyone else in Tordoch, but he used them with an earnest innocence that made them sound decent. How was he to know they weren't? He was no student of semantics, any more than that foreign girl, the wife of some literary gent, who typed a draft of that thing Lawrence wrote. Like Enrico, she assumed the gamekeeper's tetragrams were normal usage in polite society. Naturally enough, like Enrico, she brought them into her conversation to show her command of English idiom. And naturally enough she was puzzled when her husband and his cultured friends said she must never use those words again.

Not that Enrico was limited to four-letter words. Suddenly, in the same sentence, he would get his tongue round some polysyllable as if it too was a commonplace of intercourse between a man and a woman. He often misapplied and mispronounced the big word, showing he had never heard it used, but met it in print somewhere.

When that happened Granny Lyons didn't hesitate to tell him. She knew him too well and he knew her too well for any offence to be given or taken. She saw no use trying to stop him using the monosyllables he heard the natives use every time they opened their mouth. But if he was going to use big words she wanted him to get them right. He was grateful to her.

One day he spoke to her about Gerald Provan. His hands tried to help his tongue and his big brown eyes were sad.

'He's a perpernicious youth,' he ended.

'That's very good,' she commended him. 'But just say pernicious. I must tell my nephew what you said. He'll like it. He had the same opinion when he taught that boy. Aye, and there's a lot more like him he's still teaching, poor man.'

'Your nephew not happy in that school?' he lilted.

Eyebrows up. Eyes popping. Polite surprise. He shrugged and answered himself.

'No, I suppose no. Who could be?'

He shook his head slowly to indicate defeat, exhaled wearily through pursed lips, and murmured inoffensively,

'Shower of fucking bastards, that's all they are. I know them.'

He was not without self-esteem. He believed he was superior to the autochthonous tribes he served.

'They come in here and they look down on Enrico,' he complained to her. 'They call me a tally. They say, hey, tally-wally! Hey, you, Nello!'

He snapped his fingers, acting customers calling him.

'Like you call a dog. I leave Naples with my father. Me? Just a baby. We come to Scotland. Then the war. My father? Taken away. His own kind, his own kind mind you, frightened him. He had to join something. I don't know what. I know politics never his care. But the police have his name. So. Interment they say. He goes down in the Andorra Star. My mother? She live. Somehow. She work hard. Brings me up. I never much go to the school. But I work. I learn by ear. My mother and me, we speak our father's language at home. I marry. I have family. I come out here. Open my own shop. Me. Enrico Ianello from Naples. I have no boss. Ianello's boss is Enrico. Poor boy makes it good. I speak their language. Can they speak mine? Speak mine? They can't even speak their own fucking language.'

'That's very true,' said Granny Lyons.

'But yet still they look down on Enrico. I ask you. Tell me. The other night I say to that Poggy one, don't be so obstreperous. Says he to me, what the fucking hell you mean, mac. Says I to him, you mac not me. All you Scotch fucking macs. Not clever there, me. He put a great big bloody brick my window that night. That's three times in four months my window in.'

'They're getting worse,' said Granny Lyons. 'I've had mine in twice since Christmas.'

'A shop, well,' he granted. His hands moved to say there were some things you had to put up with in this world. 'But not a house.'

'But I'm on the ground floor, you know,' said Granny Lyons. 'At a bad corner too. I wouldn't mind getting a room right at the top of one of those thirtytwo storey flats they're building now. Away from it all, well above them.'

'You well above them all right,' said Enrico.

He told her about his new juke-box.

'Biggest mistake of my life,' he wailed. 'Pay for itself in a month says the man. Will bring in the young ones. Oh, big deal! Yes, brings them in too damn true. And in one night they drink what? One coffee, one coke. And what do I get? The sound of noise all night. I like hear singing. I sing myself. My father too. My mother tells me. Fine voice. You know, Italian. Not what these ignorant bastards go for.'

And indeed she knew he loved the bel canto. Often in an afternoon when the shop was quiet because the boys and girls were at school, she would go in to hear him singing in the back-scullery as he prepared ice-lollies for the fridge. He was Manrico singing farewell to his Leonora, the Duke singing about the mobility of women, or Cavaradossi singing that the stars were shining.

When she heard him enjoying himself like that with his untrained tenor, she was moved to affection for him and made no sound till he finished his aria. Then she would sing out and he would come and chat with her. She would put her old-fashioned handbag on the counter and rest her forearms across the straps, hardly holding them. She was at peace in a calm oasis somewhere between the desert of three and four p.m., and Enrico too was carefree.

On one such afternoon their pleasant counter-talk was interrupted by the entrance of three lanky hairy youths in donkey-jackets and tight trousers. They came in hipswaying as if Enrico's cafe was a saloon in a Western and they were tough hombres on the trail who had just hitched their horses to the rail outside.

'Lucky strike,' said the first.

His mates loitered behind Granny Lyons.

'Excusa-me,' said Enrico to Granny Lyons.

He attended to his strange customers. Eyebrows raised, eyes questioning.

'Lucky strike,' repeated the gunless cowboy.

Enrico's eyebrows came down to a puzzled frown.

The cowboy tried again.

'Day ye sell Lucky Strike?'

'Ah!' said Enrico. 'American cigarettes. Some I have.'

He turned to the shelves.

'But not Lucky Strike. Chesterfield, Stuyvesant. And I have–'

Even as he began naming the brands he had in stock he had a dim feeling he was being silly. But he was that bit slow. One of the cowboys behind Granny Lyons charged at her like a football-player giving away a penalty. She tottered and teetered, lost her balance and fell. Her handbag remained on the counter. The other cowboy snatched it. The one that had asked for Lucky Strike knocked over a jar of hardboiled sweets and threw a tray of Wrigley's PK at Enrico's face. In a split second the three bandits ran out together.

Granny Lyons clawed at the counter and got back on her feet. Enrico raced out of his shop like a whippet. Granny Lyons wept and trembled.

'Oh, not again,' she whimpered. 'Not again.'

Enrico came back, a lot slower than he had gone out.

'Hopeless,' he lamented, pulling his hair. 'They dive in a close round the corner. I see them. By the time I get there, gone. Up the stairs, across the back-court, through another close? Who knows?'

'Oh well, it might have been worse,' said Granny Lyons.

Her hands quivered as she tidied her grey hairs and smoothed her coat and skirt. She felt handless without her handbag. The loss diminished her.

Enrico saw how she felt. He wept in vexation.

'It's as well I was here,' she comforted him. 'Or it might have been the till they tried. And God knows what they might have done to you if you'd been alone. Lucky it was only me. They didn't get much. My God. Let them ask for it if they're that hard-up and I'll give them it.'

'I give in,' said Enrico.

He wiped his brimming brown eyes with the cuff of his white jacket.

It may have been the saying of it made him think of surrender, or he may only have been saying what he wouldn't admit before. But from that day he lost heart. He was ashamed of his shop. He hadn't the spirit to fight its invaders any longer. He was sick of non-paying customers, bullies and rioters. The booths where he had hoped to encourage a cafe-society of young people discussing politics and literature and foreign affairs were an offence to the eye. The woodwork was hacked and scratched, the walls were defaced with the sprawling initials of his patrons, the floor was fouled with discarded wads of chewing-gum. The local lads and lasses had annexed his shop as a colony for revelry and disorder. They quarrelled at the drop of a joke and fights over nothing happened every night in the week. Enrico was always expecting to see blood shed but it never quite came to that.

In an attempt to get some peace and quiet he put the juke-box out of commission. Too often it caused a fight between rival fans of different singers. But without it the boys and girls made their own noise, and that was worse.

He made a last effort to get control. One wild night some laughing youths tested the solidity of the table in the back booth by kicking it from underneath and then jumping on it from the bench. They threw crisps across the cafe and poured coke into the coffees of the mixed company in the next booth. There was a lot of recrimination, and a threat and a challenge were heard. The uproar led to some punching and wrestling and somebody got up from the floor with a knife in his hand and a nasty look in his eyes. The girls screamed, some in terror, some in delight. Enrico phoned for the police.

By the time two policemen arrived the cafe was empty except for Gerald Provan sitting in the middle booth with Poggy, having a quiet conversation with Wilma and Jennifer. Gerald wasn't intimidated by a phone-call. He knew Enrico knew what would happen if he named anybody.

Enrico told the policemen about the disturbance. He said the culprits had run away as soon as they heard him phone from the back-shop. He didn't know any of them. The boy who had drawn a knife? He had never seen him before. They were all strangers. Gerald sat back listening, his face solemn and sympathetic.

'It's a shame, Mr Ianello, so it is,' he said.

The two policemen gave Gerald and his company a hard look but said nothing. They went away. Enrico felt very foolish. After midnight his windows were smashed. For a week after that he had nuisance-calls, sometimes at one and two in the morning. The various speakers threatened him and his wife and family. One call particularly alarmed him.

'Do that again,' said the voice in the earpiece, 'and I'll cut your throat from ear to ear.'

And then the speaker laughed at him.

He was going over some bills and his bank statement one night after the shop was closed. His flat above the cafe was quiet, his wife and two children were asleep. Into the hush there moved a vague scuffling and a susurrus of hostile voices. He looked up from his counting and listened. He was always frightened until he located and interpreted what he was hearing. It was youths quarrelling in the street. He waited for them to pass. They didn't. Then his shop-door was battered and young voices were raised, calling him. He could have thought his house was on fire, the way they were carrying on. He tiptoed downstairs and stood behind the door to the street. It was double-leaved, made of stout wood, double-locked and double-bolted. He felt safe enough. They would need an axe to break in. He heard his name called again.

'En-RI-co I-a-NEL-lo!'

'Who are you?' he asked, close to the wood.

There was no answer.

Upstairs, his wife and family wakened and listened, puzzled.

'What do you want?' Enrico shouted through the wood.

He tried to sound tough and abrupt, a dangerous man to annoy.

'You,' said a bass voice, no less terrifying because it was disguised.

The appalling monosyllable was followed by a crescendo of insane screeching and hysterical laughter, male and female.

Enrico trembled in the dark. The assault on the door was renewed. He half expected it to come in, so fierce was the hammering and kicking. It didn't. But while he waited for signs of it cracking and shouted to his wife to phone the police, one of his windows had a brick through it. He pulled his hair and cursed when he heard the glass shatter. His wife screamed on her way to the phone. Then there was silence.

That was when he gave in. He made his surrender public and got his name in the papers. He had a nephew Gino who was a football-reporter on the local evening paper, and Gino put a colleague in the news-department on to it. Enrico's rambling account of his grievances was printed in an edited version.

'I cannot continue to live in this city. I must think of the safety of my wife and children. This has been building up. These people have made my life a misery with threats of violence over the phone. They have made my shop a shambles. I tried to give them service. They do not seem to want it. I am not saying where I will go. They said they will follow me if they find out.'

He went away, and nobody ever knew where, except Granny Lyons. She missed him, but she told him to go. He tried to sell his shop with the flat above it but nobody wanted that kind of shop and house in that kind of district. The abandoned cafe became a derelict site where children played, and all the metal fittings and lead guttering were stripped by nocturnal raiders.

NINETEEN

In the new session Mr Alfred was given the same class of girls again for the same three periods. He made no complaint. It was what he wanted, to keep on seeing Rose Weipers. His fondness for her became egregious. It caused talk behind his back.

'I knew none of them would ever take a crush on him,' said Mr Brown. 'But I never thought he would take a crush on one of them.'

'If it keeps him happy why should you worry?' said Mr Dale.

'I don't like it,' said Mr Brown. 'A good teacher treats all his pupils alike.'

Mr Campbell took his pipe from his mouth and put down his crossword. Clue: *View an orphan hasn't got.* It was his function in the staffroom to correct the errors of his colleagues.

'I don't know that's true,' he said. 'Pupils come in different styles. The right thing is to treat them accordingly. Not all alike. That's wrong.'

A disputation started.

'You're missing the point the lot of you,' said Mr Dale. 'If it makes him human surely it's a good thing whether it's right or wrong.'

'How can it be a good thing if it's wrong?' asked Mr Brown. 'Talk sense.'

'It depends what you mean,' said Mr Campbell. 'A good thing. What do you mean by good?'

'I mean he said good morning to me on the bus this morning,' said Mr Dale. 'Shows you how love can mellow an old crab.'

'It depends what you mean by love,' said Mr Campbell. 'If you just mean a mellowing influence, then all you're saying is a mellowing influence mellows.'

'I agree a teacher should like kids,' said Mr Brown.

'If he doesn't he's in the wrong job. But for a man to get especially fond of one pupil, above all a girl and a growing girl at that, I don't think that's right.'

'But all girls are growing girls,' said Mr Dale.

'Till they stop growing. Then they're women. And what's wrong with a man loving a woman tell me.'

'Nothing,' said Mr Brown. 'I gather it's still quite common. But that's not the point. It's a teacher loving a girl in his class we're talking about.'

'Who says he loves her?' said Mr Dale. 'Maybe he just likes her. Sure we all have a Rose. I mean, you can't help liking some kids more than others. It's only natural.'

'That's what I'm saying,' said Mr Campbell.

'You've got to define your terms. Natural, for instance. You say it's only natural. What do you mean by natural? You can have unnatural affection too you know.'

Mr Alfred came in. In his right hand he carried a poke with the two rolls brought by the Rose who had just left him. He was singing softly the words of Longfellow's translation of Müller's 'Wohin', following but never quite catching Schubert's tune.

> I know not what came o'er me,
> Nor who the counsel gave,
> But I must hasten downward,
> All with my pilgrim-stave.

He put the poke on the table and went through to the wash-hand basin.

'See, the big bugger's happy,' said Mr Dale.

'Would you grudge him it?'

'Too young a rose to pluck,' said Mr Brown.

They heard him sing louder as he turned on the taps.

> Thou has with thy soft murmur
> Murmured my senses away.

'Oh that's that thing, icht hört' ein Bächlein rauschen,' Mr Kerr announced, recitative. 'It sounds better in the German of course. You can't beat the Germans for lieder.'

'Yes, he does sound happy, doesn't he,' said Mr Campbell, and entered PANORAMA in his crossword.

Mr Alfred was indeed happy. He thought he had reason to be. Before she went away Rose let him hold her hand as usual and he stroked her hair and caressed her ear. What was new this time was, she sat on his knee for a minute. He was sitting sideways at his table, tired after being on his feet all morning. When he held out his hand for hers she was an arm's length from him. He drew her in, meaning only she should come a little nearer. She seemed to take it he meant more. She came right over and sat on one knee.

He felt the cheeks of her bottom pressed just above his kneecap. He was sure he was blushing. He was uncomfortable. He put his arm lightly round her in case she fell off, and she was so thin above the waist, she had so little on, he thought he could have counted her ribs if he had dared to squeeze her. But he didn't want to frighten her. He shifted his hand and fingered the pinna of her left ear. She drank through a straw a surplus bottle of milk left inadvertently in his classroom, and chatted about her father and family between imbibitions.

So soon does the new become a habit that in a week, when she came at lunchtime with his rolls or pies or sandwiches, she sat on his knee as a matter of course for five minutes and talked to him. She did it without any shyness, no fuss and no comment, did it calmly and casually. He was the one who felt guilty. He got into a drill of waiting for her at the door to his room and locking it swiftly when she came in. She would walk past him, slender, unsmiling, slightly splay, put the poke on the table and count out his change. By that time he had reached his chair and sat down, ready to receive her. She perched herself on his left knee, her toes just touching the floor. He was sure there must be a more comfortable position, and he was always uneasy. Yet he was disappointed any day she didn't do it.

One day she sat right across his lap. It may have been the way he was sitting or it may have been her angle of approach. But there she was. He believed her voluntary session sanctioned him to show more affection. Her legs and knees were convenient to his gangling hand, her slightly-parted thighs were settled trustingly across his. He imagined his hand moving over the unseen limbs. He would be gentle and loving. But his nerve failed. He couldn't. He thought it would be wrong. He put his arm round her waist and his hand stroked her lean flank.

'Oh Rose! I do love you!' he whispered, his mouth against her ear.

He felt at once he was silly to have said it. He tried to unsay it.

'But don't tell anybody,' he added, smiling as if it was only a joke.

He put his finger on her nose and followed the line of it down to her nostrils. To make it clear he was only teasing, he tenderly flipped a fingertip at her chin. She smiled.

Then an impulse beat him. Sitting across his lap, she was so accessible in a way she had never been when they were standing up together that he plunged at her. He kissed her, not on the mouth but on the forehead, somewhere above the right eye. It was a shot badly off target, but he felt he had done something tremendous.

Like all that had gone before the kissing too became a habit, with all the necessity of a habit. At first he kissed her only when he gave her a halfcrown at the end of the week for doing his errands. He looked forward to Fridays as payday. He was sour if anything happened to prevent his rite, as when some leech of a classmate came back with her and hung around. Usually it was Senga Provan, and he came near to disliking her as much as he had disliked her brother. To make up for those unkissing Fridays he began to kiss Rose during the week whenever he got a chance, whenever she didn't seem in a hurry away, for he needed time to create the dialogue of lovers' talk that was properly ended in a parting kiss.

Sometimes he worried over what he was doing. He was afraid she would tell her mother or a classmate. It would make him look ridiculous. Her mother might think it worse than ridiculous. She might think he was trying to entice Rose on to something wicked.

He went over it every night between waking and sleeping, recalling how his love had been born, in her sudden burst of confidence, unexpected and unpredictable, when they first met. Nobody had ever spoken to him like that before. It was she who had started their love-affair by the way she chatted to him, by her rare trusting smiles. It was all her fault. How could he refuse to love her when she urged him to it? But he believed that what she urged him to was a father's love. She was no precocious miss just trying to provoke him. She spoke to him like a daughter, and his kisses were chaste, like a father's kisses.

He loved her very name. Rose Weipers seemed no less worthy than Rose Aylmer to appear in a poem, and she herself no less possessed of 'every virtue, every grace' than that earlier Rose. But he never found time to write a poem to or about her, though he kept on intending to consecrate some faultless lines to his love for her. He settled for making her name his talisman, a pious and even apotrapaic ejaculation in moments of temptation. When he was accosted after the last pub of his nightly crawl was closed, or when he found himself in Blythswood Square or Hope Street, not drunk and yet not sober, he remembered Rose and said her name aloud to the darkness. He believed she would be shocked, or at least disappointed, if she saw him go off with a woman who had to be paid. The fact that she couldn't know what he did made no difference. She was to him like God, who knows and sees all things, even our most secret thoughts. So he never went with even the youngest prostitute he met. Rose was the only person he wanted.

Day and night he was the victim of his autumnal love, a love that seemed at one and the same time to exclude and include the possibility of sexual pleasure. Rose, its only object, had to be female or he could never have fallen in love with her. He could never have loved a boy her age. The idea disgusted him. He knew boys too well. He thought paederasty ugly. But Rose had a girl's face, not a boy's face, a girl's body, not a boy's. That was why he could love her. Yet he had no desire to proceed beyond his constant awareness of her sex. The awareness was its own pleasure. A boy could never have interested him. His love was a heterosexual love. Therefore a normal love. To love Rose seemed natural and pure in a way that loving a boy would never have seemed to him.

He was pursuing these meditations round the alcoholic confusion of his skull one night when he was importuned on his way home after the pubs were shut. He knew he ought to have gone straight for a bus instead of wandering about to ask for encounters he didn't want.

'Looking for someone?' she said pleasantly, suddenly in front of him.

He put his palms under her elbows, rocking and beaming.

'No rose in all the world, until you came,' he sang into her powdered face.

Then dried up and lurched away.

She gaped after him. She was fed up with men who mooched round dark streets and loitered in doorways and closes and floated off when she spoke to them.

'Away hame, ya stupit big bastard!' she shouted after him.

TWENTY

Rose Weipers leaned against a wash-hand basin in the girls' toilet at morning-break whispering with Senga Provan. They had agreed to stop going to the playground. To walk there was like wandering across a battlefield where Amazons ignored the rights of non-combatants and blithely mowed them down. They wanted a quiet corner and the chance of a confidential talk.

'I get right fed up with the pair of them at times,' Senga was saying. 'You'd think, my goodness it's years ago now, you'd think they'd forget it.'

Wanda Clouston, a mammose wench in third year, waddled to the door of a cubicle and tore a yard of toilet-paper from the fixture. Flushed with hebetic vulgarity she draped the streamer round Rose Weiper's neck and made to kiss her on both cheeks in a gallic award.

Rose recoiled.

'Aw, for Christ's sake,' she said. 'Be your age.'

She scattered the paper with a cross hand and smacked Wanda. Wanda pulled her hair. They wrestled. Wanda broke away, getting the worst of it, and delved a hand under her blouse.

'Ach, you! You've bust ma bra, ya bitch!' she yelled.

'It's no' a bra you need,' said Rose, still cross. 'It's a couple of hammocks.'

'Think you're somebody?' Wanda asked. Bellona.

'Ignore her, Rose,' said Senga. Grave-eyed Pallas Athene, goddess of good counsel. 'I wouldn't demean myself talking to the likes of her.'

Rose looked straight into Wanda's rash eyes. A petrifying Medusa. Wanda turned, sniffed, and waddled off.

'Think because your big sister goes wi' a toffee-boy,' she muttered vaguely.

'You see, I made a mistake,' Senga said. 'As I was saying when I was so rudely interrupted. You'd think they'd forget it. I happened to say he was all right. He could make a joke now and then. I quite liked him. You should have heard them! You'd have thought they were going to put me out the house.'

'You should never take school home,' said Rose. 'I never do.'

'But it was them raised his name first,' said Senga. 'They make me sick. Every night. How's that big dope, says Gerry. And my mother, she's not a bit better. Just because he once tried to belt her darling boy. Calls him a mean-minded big bully.'

'I could tell her he's not mean,' said Rose. 'He gives me half-a-crown every week. Sometimes more. Just for going down to the shops for him.'

'I don't like taking money from teachers,' said Senga. 'I always feel they can't afford it. Especially Alf. Did you ever look at his shoes?'

'It would hurt him if I refused,' said Rose. 'That's what I feel.'

'He's a daft big lump,' said Senga. 'Remember the morning he walked in wearing one brown shoe and one black? I bet he had a hangover. They say he's a terrible drinker. Anyway, it showed he's got two pairs of shoes. But neither of them's any good.'

'I've sometimes smelled drink on him,' said Rose.

'Can't say I have,' said Senga. 'I just know what they say.'

'It's when I go back and the room's empty,' said Rose, 'and I'm right close to him.'

'Of course,' said Senga. 'I think he likes you.'

'You know what he said to me once?' said Rose.

'No,' said Senga. 'What?'

'If I was an orphan he'd adopt me.'

They smiled together.

'O-la!' said Senga. 'I'd hate to live in the same house as a teacher.'

'When he gives me the half-crown,' said Rose, 'you know what he does?'

'No,' said Senga. 'What does he do?'

'He gives me a wee kiss,' said Rose. 'I feel right daft, the way he does it. It's not a smacker. Not even on my cheek. It's a kind of peck at my forehead. But what can I do? I'd hate to hurt him.'

'I wish somebody liked me that much,' said Senga.

'I can remember my dad used to kiss me like that at bedtime. When I was wee. But then he went away. Sometimes I don't wonder.'

'I can just see my dad kissing any of us,' said Rose. 'Mind you, he's not bad. Even when he comes in with a drink on him on a Saturday night he's not drunk. I suppose he's fond of us all right. I know he thinks the world of Martha.'

'Martha's a lovely girl,' said Senga. 'Anybody would know you two were sisters. It's just Martha's hair is different. It's really gorgeous.'

'Funny thing,' said Rose. 'Talking about kissing. You know, I've never seen my dad kiss my mum.'

The bell rang and they snailed out. Wanda slipped stealthily behind them, kicked Rose on the bottom and bounced off to her line. Rose turned to identify the assailant and sighed patiently.

She didn't mean to be disloyal when she told Senga Mr Alfred had a habit of kissing her. She didn't mean anything. She was only talking. Perhaps she had an urge to boast she had an elderly admirer, perhaps it was the intimacy induced by a tête-à-tête in the toilet made her say too much.

Whatever its reason, her casual confidence to Senga had a result neither of them expected. Senga wasn't exaggerating when she said her mother and brother were always on about Mr Alfred. They were at it again that night. She had made a mixed grill of bacon, egg, sausages, and black-pudding for tea, although she herself had no appetite. She was in the middle of a difficult period. She felt sick of living and eating. The only person who gave her any sympathy was Rose Weipers. She had vowed to be faithful to Rose for ever. And since Rose was Mr Alfred's favourite, she was committed to defending Mr Alfred too.

At first she said the minimum when she was asked as usual about the day's events at school. She knew they were hoping she would bring home some grievance that would let them make another complaint about Mr Alfred. Her inscrutable crosseyed face concealed how much the idea amused her, and the brevity of her answers made Gerald determined to annoy her.

'You mean to say he hasn't strapped you yet for nothing?' he said.

'That's right,' said Senga.

'It's only because he's feart,' said Gerald. 'He knows what would happen now if he did.'

'He knows better than to put a finger on a Provan,' said Mrs Provan. 'That's why.'

'Aye, we sorted that big bastard all right, didn't we, maw?' said Gerald.

'That's not a nice word,' said Senga.

'He's not a nice man,' said Mrs Provan.

'He's just as nice as anybody else,' said Senga. 'Nicer than some I could mention. Anyway, all the girls in my class like him.'

She knew she was getting heated, she knew she was liable to be provoked into some indiscreet remark if they heckled her too much, but she couldn't stop herself.

'Ho-ho, she's going to start a fan club for big Alfy,' said Gerald.

He laughed. With a lycorexia that offended her he forked bits of bacon, egg, and black-pudding together and bent his nuzzle over his plate as he shoved them into his wide mouth.

'I don't need to start anything,' said Senga.

'Well, don't,' said Mrs Provan. 'I don't want that man's name raised in this house.'

'It's you keeps on raising it,' said Senga. 'You say he's mean. That's one thing he's not.'

'Oh?' said Mrs Provan. 'Who says so?'

'Rose Weipers,' said Senga. 'He gives her money every

week. Just for going to a shop for him.'

'Oh yes?' said Mrs Provan.

'He treats her like a father,' said Senga. 'Something I haven't got.'

'That's enough,' said Mrs Provan.

'If she had no father,' said Senga, 'he'd take her home he said.'

'He'd what?' said Mrs Provan.

'Adopt her,' said Senga. 'Of course you wouldn't understand. Somebody being fond of somebody. Him kissing her, you'd think he was just a sloppy old man. The idea of affection, of anyone showing affection I mean. It would never occur to you two.'

'Kissing Rose Weipers?' said Gerald. 'Haw, maw! Did you hear that? Big Alfy kissing the girls and giving them money. The dirty old man!'

'I heard her,' said Mrs Provan.

'Ee-ya! Rose Weipers!' Gerald howled.

He gloated over the name with teenage lust, a loaded fork at his mouth.

'And who's Rose Weipers, tell me,' said Mrs Provan.

'Martha Weiper's wee sister,' said Gerald. 'You must have seen Martha, maw. She's the talk of the district. Doing a line with a toff student lives in wan o' the big hooses oot in Old Tordoch. A right wee snob, so she is.'

'She's not,' said Senga.

'She's a smashing blonde, maw,' said Gerald. 'Rose is no' a blonde but she's a good-looking wee bit. They're both sexy dames.'

'I understand,' said Mrs Provan.

Gerald leaned across the table and flicked a finger under Senga's nose to hit her plumb between the nostrils.

'I bet he doesn't kiss you,' he said.

'I never said he kissed Rose Weipers,' Senga wriggled. 'All I said was if he did what you two would think.'

'He's a dirty old man, isn't he, maw?' said Gerald.

'He's not a man should be teaching girls,' said Mrs Provan. 'And I'm the very one will let that be known.'

Senga wept.

'You keep out of it,' she wailed.

'Don't worry,' said her mother. 'I'll keep out of it all right.'

TWENTYONE

Mr Briggs read them both twice, the Director's letter and the enclosure, the one leading him to the other, forward and backward.

'Oh, my God! Not that man again!' he cried.

He handed them to Miss Ancill. She was always with him first thing in the morning. She opened his mail, gave it to him in descending order of importance, and stood by in case he needed her help while he took it in.

The senior members of his staff resented not so much the confidence he put in Miss Ancill as the confidences he gave her. They didn't mind her opening his mail if that was part of her job. What they didn't like was his habit of discussing it with her, of making her his chief counsellor in every problem and the first recipient of his intentions concerning administration and staffing. She had only a diploma in shorthand and typing, but they had an Honours degree in this and that, and some of them had double degrees in Arts and Science. They thought they had a higher claim to be consulted.

But Mr Briggs always needed Miss Ancill at his side when he dealt with his correspondence. After all, she was his secretary. She was there for him to talk to. He couldn't think unless he was talking. And in time of trouble he liked talking to a woman.

'What am I to do about that, tell me,' he said.

'There's a problem.'

Miss Ancill of course had read the Director's letter and the enclosure when she opened the mail before Mr Briggs came in. But she read them again as if she hadn't, taking her time, very slow and very serious. The Director's letter asked the headmaster for a prompt investigation and report on the charges contained in the accompanying anonymous complaint which accused Mr Alfred of giving money to girls in the school and using indecent practices with them, particularly one Rose Weipers. The anonymous letter was a rambling piece of vernacular prose without punctuation. Some words were badly misspelled. But the errors were so uncommon they seemed to arise from the writer's desire to support anonymity by bogus solecisms.

Miss Ancill wrinkled her nose the way anyone does at a bad smell.

'I don't believe it,' she said. 'Mr Alfred? Never! When could he do these,' she quoted distastefully, 'these "indecent practices"? Where? It's a piece of nonsense.'

'I can't imagine it myself,' said Mr Briggs. 'But I've got to make sure. I can't just ignore the Director's letter. I'll have to ask questions. Oh dear! The trouble that man has given me! If this gets in the papers it will put me in a fine position!'

Miss Ancill advised him to call in Mr Brown and Mr Campbell for a conference.

'I'd question the girl first,' said Mr Campbell.

'Mind you,' said Mr Brown. 'I don't believe there's anything in it. But I must say I think he has brought this on himself. He has been far too thick with one girl at least.'

'Oh yes?' said Mr Briggs.

'Rose Weipers,' said Mr Brown. 'The very one named. He had her in his room every day at lunchtime. And he locks the door. He doesn't know, but I've seen him.'

'There's your where and when answered,' said Mr Briggs sadly to Miss Ancill.

'Let's get this girl Weipers in,' said Mr Campbell.

'Get the truth out of her, and you'll get a line on the others.'

'If any,' said Miss Ancill.

'I'm not questioning any girl alone on a thing like this,' said Mr Briggs. 'That could put me in the cart too. Improper talk alone with a schoolgirl? No, thanks. I'll have her mother here.'

'Yes, I think you should,' said Miss Ancill.

'Or her father,' said Mr Brown.

'Or both,' said Mr Campbell.

'Just the mother, I think,' said Miss Ancill.

The attendance-officer opportunely arrived and was immediately sent away again to tell Mrs Weipers to come to the school at once on an urgent matter.

'All we can do now is wait,' said Mr Briggs. 'I expect we'll have the Director or one of his Deputies out here sometime today. I'd better have something definite for him. Because if that letter's true, well, it's a very serious business. There will have to be official action rightaway.'

'I've never known a teacher suspended on the spot,' said Mr Brown. 'Quite an event, eh?'

He clapped his hands and rubbed them.

Rose's mother came in bewildered, ushered by the janitor. Jean toddled plumply at her heels.

'I had to bring the wean,' Mrs Weipers said.

She looked at the three grave men and the single woman. They frightened her.

'I'm sorry,' she said humbly. 'But I've no one to look after her.'

Jean, aged three when Martha mentioned her to Graeme Roy, was now turned five and waiting to be admitted to the infant-school when the new session started. She ambled round Mr Brigg's room, stopped at a shelf of specimen-copies and pulled the books out one by one to use them as building-bricks. She dropped one.

'Jean! Behave yourself, you!' Mrs Weipers said. A worried woman. Not well.

She rose, stooped, and dragged Jean over beside her.

When they were both settled Mr Briggs resumed the explanation Jean had interrupted. But he was so indirect and allusive that Mrs Weipers wasn't sure if he was telling her Rose had been assaulted by a teacher or a teacher had been improperly approached by Rose. When she was thoroughly confused he gave her the anonymous letter to read.

'You'll understand why I had to send for you,' he said, going on talking even as she was trying to make it out.

She was a poor reader at the best of times, with the best of print, and the scrawly handwriting, bad spelling and lack of stops made it trebly difficult for her.

'Oh my goodness,' she whispered when she took in the meaning of 'indesent praktises'.

'I'll have to question Rose,' said Mr Briggs. 'It's my duty. I can't ignore such a terrible letter. And I'm sure you'll want to exercise your right to be present.'

Rose was as baffled as her mother. When she saw the drift of the headmaster's questions she froze. At first she said she hardly knew Mr Alfred. She only got him three periods a week. Mr Briggs asked about money. She admitted Mr Alfred sometimes gave her money. Mr Briggs asked how often. She said once a week. She didn't like the way he kept glancing at a piece of pale-blue notepaper. She guessed somebody had written something that wasn't nice about her and Mr Alfred. The girls were always writing something about somebody.

'But why should he give you money every week?' Mr Briggs asked.

He pretended he was puzzled.

'It's for going to the shops for him,' said Rose.

'Just for going errands for him, you mean?' said Mr Briggs. 'And that's all? He doesn't ask you to do anything else when you come back? When you're alone.'

'No,' she said.

She was only beginning to see what he was thinking. There were tears in her eyes. Her lower lip was wobbling.

'Did you tell anybody Mr Alfred was giving you money?' Mr Briggs encouraged her to speak.

'Yes,' said Rose. 'I told Senga Provan.'

'I see,' said Mr Briggs.

He wagged his head wisely.

'It was no girl wrote that letter,' said Mrs Weipers.

Rose was just as intelligent as any headmaster. She saw it the moment Mr Briggs saw it. If that bit of pale-blue paper wasn't the usual scribbling of some girl in her class but a letter from outside she knew how it came to be written. And remembering what else she had told Senga she hurried to get her story in before she was asked any more questions about things that seemed to be known anyway.

'I told her he kissed me,' she said. 'But I just made that up.'

'Are you sure?' Mr Briggs asked. 'That's rather hard to believe. A sensible girl like you. Why on earth should you do that?'

The brimming tears overflowed. She began to cry. She knew it made her look guilty, but she couldn't help it. Mr Briggs went on probing. If she had made it up she had been very naughty, telling lies about her teacher. But was she telling the truth now? He kept at her. Was she quite sure Mr Alfred had never kissed her?

Rose blubbered. She nodded her head and shook her head, not knowing what she was doing. All she knew was she couldn't speak. Mr Briggs watched and relaxed. He had plenty of experience in asking questions and assessing witnesses. He saw through Rose. He knew why she wept. He saw the innocence in her that had heard of evil but never met it. He was convinced the charges in the anonymous letter were false. But he was curious about Mr Alfred's behaviour. He took his time. He let the mother have a word.

'Don't be frightened, Rose,' said Mrs Weipers. 'Your mammy's here. Tell the master the truth.'

Rose admitted Mr Alfred had kissed her. Yes, often.

'At first he just held my hand!' she tried to suggest how things start and then you can't stop them.

She couldn't explain it better for crying. She wept for herself and for Mr Alfred too. She hated them all, even her mother, for finding out Mr Alfred loved her.

'What kind of a kiss?' said Mr Briggs.

'Just on my brow,' said Rose. 'It was nothing. I hardly knew.'

'Did he ever lift your dress?' said Mr Briggs. 'Even once.'

Rose turned to her mother to hide her face on the breast that had nursed her.

'No, no!' she screamed.

'Wheesht,' said Mrs Weipers.

Jean began to cry and tried to hug Rose round the legs.

'Did he ever touch you?' said Mr Briggs. 'Anywhere he shouldn't, I mean.'

Rose shook her head.

'Some of these people,' said Mrs Weipers. She stroked Rose's thick untidy hair from crown to nape as Mr Alfred had often done. 'If they have anything to say why can't they come out into the open and say it? Wheesht, ma wee hen! Your ma knows you're a good girl.'

Mr Briggs apologised.

'It's an unpleasant task, Mrs Weipers,' he said. 'But it had to be done. I'm sure you would be the first to agree we can't afford the least suspicion that a girl of Rose's age could come to any harm here. Even an anonymous letter, it's got to be investigated.'

'The fire's the place for it,' said Mrs Weipers. 'Not a word of truth in it, not a scrap of evidence.'

He spoke to Mr Alfred alone later. He didn't ask him what he had been doing. He told him. He told him he had seen Rose and her mother and knew he had been kissing the girl and giving her money. He let him see the anonymous letter and gave him some fatherly advice though he was the younger man.

He sprawled back in his swivel-chair to set the tone of an informal, friendly chat. Mr Alfred sagged before him in a position vaguely suggesting a soldier standing to attention before a superior officer.

It would be a bad thing, Mr Briggs said, if one had a class with nobody in it one could like. To find that some pupils were loveable was one of the rewards of poorly-paid profession, though one was very properly shy of mentioning love. But there must be no favouritism. It was a bad teacher that had favourites. If one found oneself becoming fond of one pupil in particular one must force oneself to give more attention to other pupils, who were probably more in need of affection. It was a bad thing to allow oneself to be emotionally involved. A bachelor was sometimes prone to do that. A man with a family would find it easier to maintain a sense of proportion. He would know girls could be little devils as well as angels. One mustn't see girls through rose-tinted spectacles. He apologised for the pun. He hadn't intended it. They could be as nasty as boys, yes, and even nastier. He could tell Mr Alfred things about girls that would shock him, things he had learnt as headmaster of a mixed comprehensive school, the things girls wrote on the lavatory walls for example. Worse than boys. It was a pity Mr Alfred wasn't married. Of course he himself and Mrs Weipers were completely satisfied there was no truth in the anonymous letter as far as Rose was concerned, and there was no other girl actually specified. The accusation that Mr Alfred was guilty of indecent practices with any girl was something neither he nor anyone else who had seen the letter believed, nonetheless . . .

He saw he had slipped there. The words 'nor anyone else who had seen the letter' made Mr Alfred wonder how many people had been shown it. Miss Ancill for one he was sure. And probably Mr Brown as Deputy Headmaster. He jerked as if prodded. He was humiliated. Once more a harsh reality had invaded the privacy of his dreams. He remembered that in the poems of his youth he had tried to negotiate with reality. But in his middle-age reality was no longer open to negotiations. It was bulldozing him. It tore up the love he had hidden under the soiled surface of his public life and heaved it aside like so much rubbish that was merely in the way of new buildings. He felt destroyed. He had no idea who had written the letter and Mr Briggs gave him no clue. All he could make of it was that Rose must have talked to somebody, somewhere, sometimes. She had wilfully made him look ridiculous.

Mr Briggs went on, man-to-man. If it came out that a teacher was in the habit of kissing a girl in his class, that could lead to many misunderstandings. Admittedly there were innocent caresses and innocent kisses. Paternal or pastoral attentions to children. But as Mr Alfred himself must be well aware Scotch reserve looked askance on kissing even between kin. And there were always people eager to make trouble, like the person who had written that malicious letter. Once they heard the word kissing they would be only too ready to impute sexual intentions to the teacher, especially if they heard the teacher was giving the girl money. In a position of trust, as every teacher was in regard to the pupils in his care, one must take great care to be like Caesar's wife.

Mr Alfred felt no ambition to be like Caesar's wife. He preferred to remain male, however inadequately. Yet while Mr Briggs was lecturing him he felt guilty enough of what he was charged with. There came into his mind the Gospel text that whosoever looketh on a woman to lust after her hath committed adultery with her already in his heart. He didn't like that text. He thought it unfair. But he knew how he had often looked on Rose. So the anonymous letter could claim the support of the Gospel for what it said about him.

He said nothing of that to Mr Briggs. He went dumbly back to his class unfit to teach again that day. He was hot with vexation, as if he had been surprised in an absurd position, like being caught in his shirt-tail and long hairy legs. His high love for Rose had been reduced to the occasion for a condescending homily from Mr Briggs, a man too discreet to kiss a growing girl who offered affection.

He stayed in town till the pubs opened. He wasn't bothered about going home. His landlady was used to his irregular returns. He drank till the pubs closed, not to get drunk but just to brood. Still, he finished up not sober and walked the streets till past midnight.

Mr Briggs had his expected visit from the Director, who wasn't inclined to judge Mr Alfred harshly. He understood him. But because of the letter it was decided to transfer him to another school.

When he saw nothing in the papers Gerald shrugged.

'Ach, don't worry, maw,' he said. 'We'll get the old bastard yet.'

TWENTYTWO

Senga heard about the letter. The whole school heard about the letter. Miss Ancill told the janitor and the janitor told the cleaners and the cleaners told the parents. But Senga knew more. She knew who had written the letter, though the writer never mentioned it.

Having made her own good guess, Rose wouldn't speak to

Senga for a week. She walked past her in the street. She changed her place in class. But Senga was too articulate to let it go on. Her hurt was great, but it would be less if she was forgiven. She waylaid Rose and had her say. She didn't waste time suggesting the writer could have been anybody. She wouldn't make a mystery where they both knew there was none. She admitted her share. She explained how a few unwise words had been picked up by Mr Alfred's enemy. She couldn't tell how sorry she was.

Her unhappiness made her eloquent. The affection that had been dammed for a week overflowed in her eyes. Rose was hard. But she couldn't quarrel. She couldn't rant and rave and accuse and denounce. She hadn't the voice for that kind of part. She listened. She gave in. They became friends again.

Still a bitterness stayed with Senga. She had sued for peace with Rose, but she waged a civil war at home. The cause of it was never alluded to by either side, though both knew what the other was thinking. The week she was in disgrace with Rose she went on a modified hunger-strike to annoy her mother. It comforted her to refuse food from an adverse party. She never missed a chance to be sarcastic. She had come to have a sharp tongue, and she used it to cut those who wounded her. Perhaps it was guilt kept her mother from using heavy artillery to discourage these bayonet-charges. Anyway she got away with them. Even Gerald had nothing much to say for a time. Senga didn't enjoy her victories. They were too easy. She wanted stiffer opposition, then she would really show what vengeance could be.

She criticised Gerald's clothes and the shoes he wore. She derided his haircut, even his walk. She mocked the way he spoke. His enunciation was poor. He swallowed half his words, he used a glottal stop, and he spoke so quickly that every sentence came over like one enormous agglutination of syllables. It pleased Senga to make him repeat what he said the few times he dared speak to her.

'Pardon. What did you say?'

She gave a demonstration of clear speech in her very question.

'We'll have less of your airs, madam,' said her mother. 'Don't you try and make a monkey out of Gerald.'

'If people can't speak properly they can't expect to be understood,' said Senga.

'Feudcleanyurears,' said Gerald.

'Pardon,' said Senga.

'Do you think there's nothing wrong with the way you speak?' said her mother, crushing her with tone and glare, ironing handkerchiefs for Gerald. 'You should hear yourself sometimes. But we're not good enough for you. Oh no! You're that superior.'

'To him and his pals anyway,' said Senga.

She was loaded with venom, ready to strike.

'There's nothing wrong with Gerald's pals,' said her mother.

'Not much,' said Senga. 'Crowd of apes.'

'Hoosapes?' said Gerald.

'And he's in a gang,' Senga tossed at her mother.

'Hoosnagang?' Gerald shouted.

'You are,' Senga turned, shouting back.

'Oh, hold your tongue, you little besom,' said her mother. 'You're aye nagging. What shirt do you want to wear tomorrow, Gerald?'

'Mayella,' said Gerald.

'You don't like the truth,' said Senga. 'Either of you.'

'Gerald sees his friends after a hard day's work,' said her mother. She flattened the last handkerchief, stacked the lot. 'They go out and enjoy themselves, and you choose to call it a gang.'

'Because so it is,' said Senga. 'He's in a gang all right. I'm telling you. You'll find out.'

'What gang?' her mother demanded. Voice raised. Angry. 'You let your imagination run away with you, you do.'

'Just ask him,' said Senga. 'Ask him what they call his gang.'

'Amnoinanygang,' said Gerald.

He rushed across the kitchen with fist raised to thump his sister as he used to do. Senga hurried to a corner, turned her back to him, hands at her ears, reverting to her childish kyphosis at the threat of assault.

'She's not worth it, Gerald,' said the mother. 'Just ignore her.'

But Gerald was in a gang. It was called the Cogs. Nobody knew why.

Gangs were no novelty in the city. Between the wars they did some shopbreaking and demanding money with menaces, but that was only on the side. They were never started for criminal purposes. They had no big boss in the background planning even petty crime. They were the local expression of religious sympathies amongst the irreligious. Their main activities were mutual aggression and breach of the peace. Like ancient Constantinople, the city had its factions of Blue and Green, his devotion to either depending solely on the adherent's accident of birth. There were gangs that had a special loyalty to the memory of William Prince of Orange for beating the papishes at the Boyne in 1690. There were gangs that professed a particular reverence for the Holy Father and a great dislike to King Billy. It was a matter of complete indifference to both sides that the Pope and the Orangeman were allies in that famous victory.

But now instead of the gangs that flourished in the slump, the Norman Conks, San Toy, Billy Boys and Sally Boys, Cheeky Forty, Calton Entry and Baltic Fleet, all with explicit or latent support for the Orange or the Green, there were the gangs of the affluent society, the Toi, Tong, Peg, Monks, Fleet, Gringo, Goucho, Cody, Cumbie, Town and many others.

Orange and Green no longer mattered very much, though even in a period of ecumenicity colour prejudice couldn't be entirely obliterated. It could still be heard at some football matches, where the fans believed King Billy supported the Rangers and the Pope supported Celtic. But with the decline of religion the new gangs had merely secular loyalties. They were the result of a rationalisation of production in keeping with a technological society. Instead of a district manufacturing two gangs with different colours each district turned out one gang with no colour.

The members lived like bushmen, treating anybody from a different part of the forest as if he belonged to a different species. Strangers were stopped and challenged, assaulted with boot and knife, and killed if they resisted. If no aliens turned up they went out to look for them. They went by bus and train in the summer season to the seaside resorts and county towns, travelling in the autumn as far south as Blackpool, where the natives deserved to be beaten up for not belonging to Glasgow. Between vacations they invaded each other's territory. They fought in dance-halls, pubs, the queen's highway, discotheques and corporation-parks.

The Cogs were in the news a fortnight after Senga named them. They were the budding talent of Tordoch, and it was thanks to Gerald they got headlines and Wilma got her name in the papers.

It all started at a party in Jennifer's house.

Jennifer and Wilma were amongst the dozen or so girls in the Cogs. If nothing was cooking it was the girls lit the gas. When they went dancing they would either pick a quarrel in the powder-room with any dame that looked sideways at them or they would tell the Cog-commander they had been insulted by their escort. If it came to a battle they played their part. The only weapon they used was a steel comb.

Of course nobody expected any trouble the night of Jennifer's party. They weren't out on the town looking for anything. They were all tadpoles in their own pond. Jennifer's parents were away at Ayr for the week-end visiting relatives, and Jennifer fixed a record-session. She invited a mixed company, mostly Cogs. Everyone knew she kept open house on such an occasion, and some of the boys and girls brought other guests. There must have been forty or fifty young ones in that four-roomed council house that night.

It was never found out who brought Alec McLetchie, but brought he was. He was a darkeyed boy of Gerald's age, with long chestnut hair down to the collar of his newstyle jacket. He had a broad face and a big hanging-lipped mouth. He looked just like a pop singer or one of a beat group. At least that's what Wilma thought. She was thrilled with the cut of him. She was getting tired of Gerald. His blond head seemed shallow beside the dark depths of Alec's rich waves.

The trouble was Wilma liked boys of any colour. She liked to make up to boys, to lead them on and then tease them by wriggling out of it. She was amused when she saw they were excited. It always surprised her to see how easily a boy got excited. She wanted to see if Alec was easily excited. She called him Alec rightaway to put him at his ease, because it gave her the giggles if a boy was stiff when she spoke to him. If he wasn't easily excited he might be her true mate instead of Gerald. She sat beside him on the settee when the first record was being played and clasped his hand between her left thigh and his right. She felt switched on, she felt a higher voltage coming through, she began to glow.

Jennifer's guests had brought cans of beer and bottles of coke. A young syndicate, with a simple theory of seduction, had clubbed for a bottle of vodka to go with the coke. Jennifer was disc-jockey as well as hostess. She had a good line of patter at each record and everyone was happy. The liquor flowed, the guests were all keen to show they were sophisticated in spite of the burden of being young, and the party was swinging.

Alec solemnly nuzzled Wilma and Wilma played with his chestnut hair in a five finger exercise. The fetching of drinks and the parking of empty glasses caused some irregular rising and sitting and changing of seats. After one of those moves Wilma found she was being crushed to one end of the settee by an extra occupant who shouldn't have been there. She took the chance to sit on Alec's lap. He fondled her knees and put his hand up her miniskirted thighs a little distance. Not eagerly, but rather as if going through a drill expected of him. He still looked solemn, kind of faraway, his big mouth drooping with the weight of the lower lip. But in Wilma's opinion he was smouldering like a dross fire that would burst into flame at the least touch. She put one arm round his neck, then both. Robust they were and shapely, naked from the shoulders of her sleeveless blouse. She bent her face to his, silently asking. They kissed.

Across the room at the same time Gerald was kissing Davina Gordon. She was a chubby-girl he had never met before. When they were introduced he chanted as a joke, 'A Gordon for me!' He was stuck with her after that. But he wasn't annoyed. He didn't mind what he did because she didn't. It was her first time at one of Jennifer's parties and she wanted to get invited back. But Gerald was too much for her. She was too untrained to have the stamina for his long kiss. She had to come up for air. So Gerald was idle while Wilma and Alec were still busy. He saw them mouth to mouth as if they were stuck together by a new super-adhesive. He was shocked. Her infidelity offended him. Wilma caught the dagger of his glare in a corner of her eye as she squinted to see how other lovers were getting on. She palmed Alec away, smacked his hand and lifted it from her thigh. She pulled down her skirt.

Gerald wasn't the boy to let it be smoothed over as easily as that. His honour demanded satisfaction. When the party was starting to break up at two in the morning he slipped out ahead with Poggy and Smudge and a couple more of his handers. He knew Wilma was fixed to stay overnight to keep Jennifer company and he told his mates what the situation demanded. When McLetchie came round the corner alone he was ambushed and beaten up. No weapons were used. Just five pairs of ringed fists against one, five pairs of sharp shoes on one huddled body. McLetchie went home a bruised and bloody mess and told his big brother.

And who was his big brother? He was Peter McLetchie, known as Big Paw, one of the Fangs from the Auchenglass scheme. Gerald was furious when he got the buzz.

'Who the hell brung a Fang's kid brother to Jenny's?' he asked his assembled company.

No one answered. They were all troubled in spirit. But the threat of invasion and the slogan 'Cogs!' raised them to the high pitch of dare-and-die required for battle. All they lacked was a claymore and kilts and someone to play the bagpipes. They fought long and bravely when the Fangs attacked them in the Ballochmyle Road, the main pass into the highlands of Tordoch. Gerald was working late in the garage that night and was sorry he missed it he said, but he couldn't get away. Even without him the Cogs managed to drive the Fangs away in a late rally. The buses on Ballochmyle Road were held up for twenty minutes before the fighting ended, but the police got there in time to pick up some warriors who were slow in leaving the battlefield. That was when the Cogs got headlines. SIXTEEN HELD AFTER COGS FIGHT. Wilma's turn came a few days later.

The defeat of the invasion didn't discourage Big Paw. He knew it was hard, if not impossible, to conquer someone else's territory. And he was an old hand at drag-fighting. He sent a challenge by under-ground. Let any one of those who had given his brother a doing come out on Sunday morning and he would take him on, all in. A signal was returned by the same route. Message received and understood.

Big Paw came into the Weavers Lane from the Ballochmyle Road with a posse of grim hombres. Poggy came in from the Tordoch Crescent end, with Gerald and Smudge and half-a-dozen anonymous backers behind him. Poggy enjoyed the limelight. The sun was shining. He walked slowly to Big Paw and Big Paw walked slowly to him. High Noon in the peace of a Scotch Sabbath.

'G'on, Poggy, take him,' said Gerald.

Poggy stopped, chest out, and waited. The captain's hand on his shoulder smote.

'Easy meat,' Gerald whispered. 'You can do him.'

'Fancy yer chance, day ye?' Big Paw drawled.

'Could take you anyway,' Poggy said, and spat at Big Paw's feet. 'Any time.'

It started mildly enough, just a rough-house warm-up, until Big Paw got Poggy on the ground and gave him a kicking. Poggy fumbled to get at a knife in his waistband before rising. Big Paw drew smoothly from his braces, ready for him. To save time Gerald bent quickly and shoved his own knife into Poggy's shaking hand and Poggy scrambled up with it clenched in his right fist. But Big Paw had his chisel out. And while Poggy was still trying to get balanced on his feet and make up his mind where and when and if to strike, Big Paw struck first. It was a swift, savage, powerful thrust. The whole weight of his body sent it in and down. Poggy fell down again, bleeding. Big Paw and his posse let it go at that and ran off to get a bus on the Ballochmyle Road. They knew when it was the end of a programme. No point waiting for the commercials.

Poggy pulled at his shirt. It was his best shirt. He always wore his best shirt on Sundays. It was soaked with blood. His hand was red to the wrist. He was amazed. He gasped an appeal.

'Gerry, help! Help me! That bastard, he's got me, so he has!'

But Gerald was in as big a hurry as the other fellow.

'Yill b'aw right,' he shouted over his shoulder. 'Hang on! Ah'll phone fur a namblance.'

He decamped with Smudge and the rest of the backers.

Poggy died alone there in the Weavers Lane that quiet Sunday morning under a clear sky. The only person who got any pleasure out of the business was Wilma. When the pressmen came into Tordoch looking for a story she gave them one. She said Poggy had been her boyfriend. She told them she had foolishly tried to make him jealous by letting another boy kiss her at a party. The two boys had gone and had this fight over her. She was heart-broken it ever happened. She would never forget Poggy. He was a kind, gentle boy.

'IT'S ALL MY FAULT' said the thirtytwo point caption above a picture of her smiling pretty face. She cut it out and kept it with a bundle of holiday-snaps in her handbag.

PART TWO

The Writing on the Wall

TWENTYTHREE

Mr Alfred didn't like his new school. The old journey to Collinsburn was long enough, but this was twice as long. He had to change buses in the city centre, and if he missed one by a few seconds he had a long wait for another. It meant he had to rise a lot earlier to allow for delays. He soldiered glumly on, suffering life patiently.

He was still in mourning for the loss of Rose. Even before he left Collinsburn she was taken from him. There was a quick alteration made in his timetable and someone else was given her class till his transfer came through. He gained free-time by the adjustment, but that was no compensation. He still felt she had treated him badly, and yet he wanted to see her again. He hoped for her every day, but she never came near him.

Rather than tell his aunt the truth he said he had asked for a transfer.

'You were always saying that's what I should do,' he reminded her.

'It took you a long time,' said Granny Lyons. 'And why so sudden? Are you sure there's not something behind it you're not telling?'

'No, nothing,' he said. 'I just got fed up with Tordoch. That's all. Collinsburn used to be a good school, but not any longer.'

He changed the subject. He was afraid he would give himself away if he said any more.

The transfer made his visits to her less frequent than ever. If any of his old pupils saw him in Tordoch any night they would think he was looking for Rose. That's how he saw it, for he believed his love was common knowledge. He believed a rumour of it had preceded him to his new school. He knew his very appearance when he entered the staffroom for the first time would make him seem an oddity. He was sure the teachers already there saw him as a tall, grey, haggard old man who came sidling in unsociably. And he was sure they talked about him behind his back and said a man of his age wouldn't be shifted from one school to another unless he was no use at his job.

He took more and more to drink in the evenings. He found he had to drink more to get the right effect of not worrying about anything. He drank in different parts of the city, in a kind of judicial assizes, to observe the customs and customers in a variety of bars. To prevent any barmaid seeing how much he took he never spent the whole night in one pub. His circuits helped him to get over Rose. He recovered as from an illness, with diminishing relapses.

It wasn't just the tedious journey to an outlying housing-scheme made him dislike Waterholm Comprehensive, called Watty Compy by its pupils, with an *ah* and a glottal stop in the Watty. It was also the boys he had to teach. They frightened him. He had never been frightened in a classroom before.

It started the day he arrived and came to a climax at four o'clock. He left promptly because he wasn't sure about the times of the buses. He never left promptly again. A mob of boys at the stop outside the school tried to board the first bus that came. A score of them jammed the platform and the staircase to the top deck. The rest milled between the bus and the pavement. The Pakistani conductor was angry. The boys were merry. Especially to have made the conductor angry. The driver came out of his cabin and announced he wasn't going on till the surplus boys got off. The boys wouldn't get off. They were in good spirits. They jeered at the driver, they called the conductor nigger boy, they argued with the passengers.

Mr Alfred was shocked. He hated disorder and bad manners. He raised his voice. He told the boys to line up quietly in a proper queue. Nobody bothered. Nobody knew him.

'You're wasting your time, mac,' said an old-age-pensioner watching the world go by from the kerb. 'The young ones the day! They'll no' listen to anybody.'

A fresh wave of boys surged on to the platform, leaping joyously on their schoolmates' backs.

'Come on, get off!' the submerged conductor shouted. 'Some of you get off.'

The adults already on the bus grumbled at the hold-up. They said the conductor should put the boys off. They said the driver should drive on. They said they didn't know what the world was coming to. They made remarks about modern education when the boys gave in and the bus moved off.

'Makes you wonder what they learn them at the school nowadays,' said a stout lady with a labrador under the seat.

'It's all these free-travel passes,' said the conductor. 'They should take them from them. Make them walk. All I get is cheek.'

A squad of boys rang alongside the departing bus, chanting.

'Watty Compy! Cha-cha-cha!'

They straggled behind when the bus gathered speed, and one of them picked up a stone and threw it at the conductor who was leaning from the platform giving them the v-sign Gerald had given Enrico.

Mr Alfred walked on to the next fare-stage to get away from the remnants of the mob. He was in a bad temper. He saw why he was the only teacher who had waited with the pupils for a bus. Most of his new colleagues had a car, and they had given a lift to those who hadn't. Nobody had offered him a lift. He didn't mind that, but he thought somebody should have warned him what he would walk into if he went to the stop outside the school.

He tried to settle down in Waterholm. It seemed an ugly place. He was familiar with the pupillary scribblings that raped the virgin flyleaves of textbooks. He had seen them countless times in Collinsburn and he wasn't surprised to see them in Waterholm. There was nothing new in the otiose curves intended to represent the female breasts, waist and hips, in the crude sketches of the male organ, and certainly nothing new in the four letter words whose use in print was sometimes supposed to prove the author had a literary talent never attributed to the boys who wrote them in their schoolbooks. What was new was the sheer quantity of obscene scribbling. And the quantity became quality. It gave Waterholm a peculiar aura, increasing his dislike and fear of it.

What was also new, and what puzzled him, was the frequent occurrence of the word 'Hox'. He saw it everywhere in Waterholm. In textbooks, in exercise books, cut on the desks, scratched on the twelve-inch rules, pencilled in the corridors. The janitor told him it was in the lavatories too, chalked on the walls scrawled in the cubicles, chiselled on the doors. Sometimes it was 'Yung Hox'.

He unfroze far enough to ask what it meant when he was alone in the staffroom with a brighteyed tubby little man known to the boys as Wee Bobby. This was Harry Murdoch, a man of Mr Alfred's age. Though unknown to Mr Alfred he had been his contemporary at university, and like him had taken an ordinary degree in Arts and trained for teaching. The day Mr Alfred arrived at Waterholm he recognised him as the student who had been famous for the amount of poetry he contributed to the university magazine. Murdoch had found the poems unreadable, but in middle-age he was willing to be pleasant to a contemporary. He laughed agreeably at Mr Alfred's question.

'Hox?' he said, echoing Mr Alfred's precise rhyming of it with Box and Cox. 'It's really Hawks. That's our local mob.'

'Mob?' said Mr Alfred, disliking the word.

'Gang,' said Mr Murdoch. 'The boys here call themselves the Young Hawks. All these gangs, they put their name up. There's hardly a blank wall anywhere now. Haven't you noticed?'

'Can't say I have,' said Mr Alfred.

'You must know the Cogs,' said Mr Murdoch.

'Cogs?' said Mr Alfred.

'Don't tell me you don't know the Cogs,' said Mr Murdoch. 'You must have seen the name on the walls when you were in Tordoch.'

Mr Alfred said he hadn't.

'They were in the papers not long ago,' said Mr Murdoch. 'A lad was knifed in a Cog fight. It happens every day. There's always somebody knifing somebody now. You should keep up with current affairs.'

He wanted to drop the topic and ask Mr Alfred if he still wrote any poetry. But he was afraid the question might sound derisive instead of friendly. And he wanted to be friendly, but Mr Alfred's face put him off. So he said nothing. At the same moment Mr Alfred wanted to ask him why the boys called him Wee Bobby when his name was Harry. But he didn't want to seem nosey. So he said nothing either. Yet in their silence there was the respect of one old soldier for another.

TWENTYFOUR

Mr Alfred took Harry Murdoch's advice. He tried to keep up with current affairs. He began to read a morning-paper, which was more than he had done when Rose brought him one every day at lunchtime. Buying something she used to get for him was only one of the many trivial acts that resurrected her. It made him wish he could go back over the script of his life and rewrite the dialogue. But he knew he had no option. He had to read the part he had been given.

Travelling across the city on a route not yet stale to him he would glance from his paper to see where the bus was going. Every day from the top-deck he saw another gang-name on the walls and hoardings. Every day he read of another boy of seventeen knifing a boy of eighteen or vice versa. His route and his paper told him he had been missing all Murdoch took for granted.

He saw a new rash break out on the scarred face of the city. Wherever the name of a gang was scribbled the words YA BASS were added. The application of the phrase caused some dispute at first. Nobody doubted YA BASS meant YOU BASTARD. But the grammarians who discussed it were undecided about its vocative or apostrophic use. Some said COGS YA BASS meant O COGS! YOU ARE BASTARDS! Others said it meant WE ARE THE COGS, O YOU BASTARDS! A fifteen-year-old boy charged with assault and breach of the peace, and also with daubing TONGS YA BASS on a bus-shelter, said in court that YA BASS was an Italian phrase meaning FOR EVER. But the sheriff didn't believe him.

Some of the intelligentsia seemed to believe him. Following a fashion, as the intelligentsia often do, they wrote the names of miscellaneous culture-heroes in public places and added YA BASS. Thus soon after the original examples of COGS YA BASS, TOI YA BASS, TONGS YA BASS, FLEET YA BASS, and so on, which were plastered all over the districts where those gangs lived, a secondary epidemic occurred on certain sites only. SHELLEY YA BASS suddenly appeared in the basement of the University Union. In a public-convenience near the Mitchell Library MARX YA BASS was scrawled in one hand, LENIN YA BASS in another, and TROTSKY YA BASS in a third. When *The Caretaker* was put on at the King's Theatre PINTER YA BASS was pencilled on a poster in the foyer. BECKETT YA BASS, later and more familiarly SAM YA BASS, was scribbled on the wall of a public-house urinal near the Citizens' Theatre the week *Happy Days* was on. When the same theatre presented *Ghosts* somebody managed to write IBSEN YA BASS in large capitals on the staircase to the dress-circle.

In bus-shelters, railway-stations and tenement closes, on factory-walls and shop-fronts, on telephone-boxes, junction-boxes, police-boxes and pillar-boxes, outside churches, libraries, offices, schools and warehouses, on the back of the seats upstairs on the buses, with the rexine ripped off to show plain wood, wherever there was a wall or a hoarding, a gang-name and YA BASS were flaunted. Always in big clumsy capitals, in white paint, in yellow paint, in green pencil, in blue pencil, in black ink and purple ink. The more recently a surface was cleaned or repainted the more immediate the writing.

Mr Alfred was puzzled.

'When do they do it?' he asked. 'What do they use?'

'A paint-spray,' said Harry Murdoch. 'Or a felt-pen.'

'I'm surprised nobody is ever caught doing it,' said Mr Alfred.

'Maybe it's leprechauns. Or monsters from outer space. You know, psychological warfare. Demoralise us before they invade in force.'

Murdoch laughed at his passing fancy but Mr Alfred wasn't amused. The rash seemed to him so mysterious he was ready to believe anything. It upset him. He used his pubcrawls to make a perlustration of the city, north and south of the river, east and west of the Square. He began to compile a list of what he saw. The words weren't inspired graffiti. They weren't the poetry and pathos photographed and commented on by two young Londoners to make up a book at a couple of guineas. They weren't political or surrealist, they weren't witty or comic. They were only the monotonous evidence of a civic battology. He brooded over the inexplicable words that turned up irregularly alongside YA BASS. He noted FUZZ, JOEY, DOTT, PEEM, MUSHY, BUNNY, ETTIE, CLAN, BIM and forty more. Sometimes the gang-name was followed by OK instead of YA BASS, sometimes it was preceded by YY, but he couldn't find out what YY meant.

He became obsessed with the unending defacement of the city. He was angry nobody seemed to care, nobody did anything about it. The correspondence columns of the papers were filled with debates about the need for comprehensive schools and a technological education in a twentieth-century Britain, about the duty of adults to hand on a moral code and maintain the nation's cultural heritage, about the prevalence of bad language in television plays. But never a word about the writing on the wall. He made himself irritable, worrying. Harry Murdoch laughed at him. He said 'Ya Bass' was a contribution to Scottish literature. It was even used as a joke in one of the pantomimes.

'There's a housing-sketch about the multistorey flats,' he explained. 'And the dame does a solo piece in the old panto couplets. Something like,

If you're a stranger in Auchenglass
Just shout the password, Fangs ya bass!

It brings the house down they tell me.'

Mr Alfred was shocked.

Meanwhile, his attempt to make the best of Waterholm and forget Rose wasn't very successful. He couldn't get much work done with the classes he was given. They seemed barely literate. He had Murdoch's registration-class for two periods every day and he risked a comment since Murdoch was the only man on the staff he cared to talk to.

'I'm finding it hard to do much with your fellows,' he said. 'I can't get anywhere.'

'Don't worry, old boy,' said Murdoch. 'Neither can I. We're out of date, you and me, with our M.A. Ordinary. After thirty years in the job we've no future. We don't rank in a Comprehensive, so we get the worst classes.'

He smiled. He wasn't bitter. He did what he could to teach some maths, went home, and put the school out of his mind. He had his garden in the spring and summer, his classical records in the autumn and winter, and golf when the mood and weather suited.

Mr Alfred was different. He had no garden and no hobbies. He worried. Anxious to get on good terms with the boys he tried chatting to them paternally with his hands in his pockets. He would be patient and pleasant. He wouldn't get rattled. He gently discouraged a forward youngster who always wanted the limelight, he wagged a hushing finger at another who kept answering out of turn. He had seen enough to know a class could be goaded into insurrection by tyranny, clammed to sullenness by sarcasm. He wanted to be benevolent without being a despot. He wanted to be friendly and get communication. But there were no dividends from his policy. Only idleness, noise, and bad manners. That was what frightened him. He saw something uncivilised in their eyes, something rude in their smirk, something savage in their slouch. They were foreigners. They didn't speak his language. They were on a different channel and he couldn't switch over. He believed that like animals they would sense he was afraid and turn on him. He tried to hide his fear, to conquer it by a kind of auto-suggestion. He put on a free and easy manner, pretending they didn't frighten him. He failed.

Then on a Thursday morning came what he had always thought impossible. Mr Murdoch's class came to him the first period, lads of fourteen and fifteen. The team they supported had won a European Cup match the night before. Mr Alfred had seen the result in the paper, but it meant nothing to him. He didn't appreciate it was a glorious victory. So he didn't expect the entry of a choir singing the song the fans had sung the night before. He bawled at them. They went on singing. Some sat down sideways with their long legs stretched out. Others hunched round the hot pipes, fondling the warm metal, and argued with a nonconformist who said their team was lucky. Somebody played a party-tune on a mouth-organ. Two upstanding boys, as big as Mr Alfred himself, quarrelled about whose seat it was in the back row.

'Sit down there!' he roared. 'Be quiet!'

The edge on his voice made him even angrier than he was already. He knew he was getting himself worked up, but he couldn't stand the noise. The insult of an uproar in his classroom maddened him.

'Sit down! Be quiet!' he roared again.

'Sit down! Be quiet!' echoed a mocking soprano.

So sudden it was, so unexpected, he failed to pin the source. He walked in among them, up and down the passages. Young eyes looked at him with calm insolence, mouths grinned but said nothing. Feet stamped when he passed.

'Sit down there! Be quiet!' a parrot-voice squawked.

It came again. And again.

'Be quiet! Sit down! Sit down! Be quiet!'

Always from behind his back. Bass, baritone and tenor. All bogus. Putting the impossible challenge to spot who it was.

He fired glares right, left and centre. He was at bay, and he knew it. He trembled. He was ripe for murder. There came into his mind the question a colleague in Collinsburn had once put to him.

'What would you do if a whole class started kidding you?'

'It wouldn't happen,' he had answered then. 'Not to me. I wouldn't let it.'

'No, it wouldn't happen to you because they know you here,' his friend said. 'But suppose they didn't know you. Suppose it did happen. What would you do? What could you do?'

'I don't know,' he admitted. 'I can't imagine it happening to me.'

And now it had. They were jeering at him, and he could do nothing to stop them. The row they were making recalled the class that had baited the young Latin teacher next door to him a long time ago. He was humiliated to be a victim where once he had been only an observer.

At that point Mr Murdoch came in. He had heard enough outside. He knew his class as a man knows his warts or corns. He picked on one conspicuous boy even as he crossed the door.

'Hey, Jumbo! Pipe down! And get back to your seat or I'll skelp your big arse hard, so I will.'

'It's no' me, Bobby,' Jumbo shouted back. 'Ah'm daying nothing. It's him.'

He put the finger on the boy nearest him, shoved him accusingly. But he sat down. Grudgingly. Still, he sat. The class hushed in waves of gathering peace.

Mr Murdoch, brighteyed and tubby, strolled up and down the silent passages. He whispered an auricular threat here, gave a nuchal smack there, padded to the front of the class and gave Mr Alfred a wink the boys couldn't see.

'Let it rest,' he whispered on the way out. 'They won't do it again.'

In the staffroom later he told Mr Alfred not to worry. It was only because he was still a stranger. This class always chanced its arm with a new teacher, no matter how old he was. The only answer was to hit somebody hard right away. Rough justice for these fiery particles. Show them who's boss.

'But even that's failing,' he elaborated sadly. 'It used to be boys took a pride in taking the belt. They'd boast how many they got. They used to despise a man couldn't use the strap. Ach him, they'd say, he canny draw it! But now they want to argue. It wasn't me, it was him. They're yellow. They know their rights. We can't do this and we can't do that, but they can do what they like. They're outside the law. It's all this child-cult. They're starting to defy me even. I had a reputation here. Handed down. God, I taught their fathers! There was a time no boy ever dared look sideways at me. But not now. I'm losing ground. There's no respect now for tradition. I've got to act the clown, speak their lingo, to keep on the right side of them. But there are limits. I'm telling you, it will be hell let loose when they raise the leaving-age.'

Mr Alfred didn't need advice about showing who was boss. He didn't need a lecture on the change for the worse in the attitude of the pupils. He didn't need gloomy prophecies about the future. He knew all that. He had said it himself, often. Platitudes didn't stop his belly quivering with anger. He was ashamed that his class had been silenced only by a colleague's intervention. He was furious he hadn't had revenge. He wanted to hit out and assert himself. He wanted to terrorise them so much they wouldn't dare mock him again. But when Murdoch left the room all he could do was get on with his lesson, and a poor one it was. He was sick with frustrated passion. At the morning-break he went to the staffroom toilet and vomited in the wash-hand basin.

He wasn't displeased when Waterholm was raided one night in what the papers called an orgy of destruction. Gang-slogans were painted on the walls and blackboards, bottles of glue were emptied on the classroom floors, text-books and exercise books were torn up and scattered, fire hoses were turned on, flooding four classrooms, and the secretary's room and the gymnasium were damaged by fire. But the main attack was on a recent acquisition greatly valued by the headmaster. It was what he called the Language Laboratory, where a classroom had been converted into a number of cubicles with tape-recorders, headphones, and some French and German conversation on tape. The cubicles were wrecked and the sound equipment was smashed beyond repair.

Mr Alfred used the break-in to justify his dislike of the pupils of Watty Compy, for nobody doubted some of them were the culprits.

'I'm not surprised,' he said. 'That's the kind of people you have here. I though Tordoch was bad, but I see I was transferred from the Ostrogoths to the Visigoths. That's all.'

'Ah, now!' said Harry Murdoch. 'Be fair! It could happen in any school.'

TWENTYFIVE

The love-affair between Martha Weipers and Graeme Roy was over. Mr Alfred read about them in the paper at a quarter to five one evening the week before Christmas. He bought a paper in the city-centre when he changed buses. Sleet was falling and the bus-windows were misty. He couldn't see through them. All he could do was read his paper. It was the name Weipers caught his eye and gave his heart a knock. But it wasn't Rose. It was Martha. She was found dead in Graeme Roy's car at 8 a.m. She must have died in the small hours of the morning. Graeme Roy was dead beside her. He was in the driver's seat and she was leaning against him with her head across his chest. His left arm was round her shoulder. The car was in the garage at the side of his father's house. They had been at a late-night dance in the University Union and Roy's parents were asleep at the time he was expected home.

Mr Alfred went to see his aunt. It was his first visit for a long time. She knew he hadn't come just because Christmas was near. She too had seen a paper. She knew he wanted to hear what they were saying about it in Tordoch. But she knew he wouldn't ask. He would never admit he liked gossip.

'I see your old school's in the papers again,' she said.

'So long as it's not on television,' he answered her.

He spoke lightly, pretending he didn't know what she was talking about and didn't care, implying she ought to know he wasn't interested in anything to do with his old school.

'Former dux-girl at Collinsburn,' she read from the paper. 'She looks such a happy girl in that picture. You'd wonder how the papers get hold of these old photos. I thought you might have seen it.'

'No,' he said.

His lie meant he had to read the report as if he hadn't seen it before. He was ashamed of his deceit. But its purpose was to hide his true feelings. He kept thinking of Rose. He wanted to comfort her.

'You see the police think it was fumes poisoned them,' said Granny Lyons.

'That would be carbon monoxide,' said Mr. Alfred. 'If the engine was running and the doors closed. It doesn't say. Or does it?'

He acted a second reading of an account he knew by heart.

'They're saying here it was suicide,' said Granny Lyons. 'The pair of them together. Because she was in trouble.'

'There's always folk want to gossip,' said Mr Alfred. 'Folk that like to think the worst.'

'Did you know them?' asked Granny Lyons.

'I didn't know her,' he said. He wouldn't mention Rose. 'I taught the boy once. A very intelligent boy as far as I remember.'

'He couldn't have been all that intelligent,' said Granny Lyons. 'It was the girl was clever. See what it says. Prizes for French and German. But see what it says about him. He gave up his studies at the university a year ago. He must have been a right failure, him.'

'Many a boy good at school fails at university,' said Mr Alfred. 'I've known highly intelligent boys had to give it up. Not their bent.'

'Well, that wasn't very intelligent,' said Granny Lyons. 'What he did. If all they say is true.'

'If all they say is true,' said Mr Alfred. 'Suppose it is. Perhaps he loved her.'

'He took an odd way of showing it,' said Granny Lyons.

'He was young,' said Mr Alfred. 'They were both young. Perhaps they thought love was all. How can a man die better than with his loved one dead beside him? Maybe that's what he thought.'

'A strange kind of love,' said Granny Lyons, 'to want to die together. They had their whole life before them.'

'But if they saw no future?' said Mr Alfred.

The way he saw it, the death-wish was in them. He remembered he had known it himself when he first saw he would never get his poems published. But he had drawn back from suicide. Graeme Roy hadn't. That was the difference between them. What he didn't know, and knew he couldn't know, was the temptation Graeme Roy had met and what had led him into it, how great the despair imposed by age and circumstance, what defeat or resistance he had suffered from Martha, who may have chosen to die in the flesh rather than die in the Elizabethan sense. Perhaps he had lost heart because he was a university failure. Perhaps his parents had forbidden any talk of marriage till he qualified for some profession. Or even forbidden him to see Martha at all because she lived in the worst street in Tordoch. Then it was a worldly ban had made him choose eternity and take Martha with him.

He brooded over them. Over Martha too young to die and over Roy persuading her death was life's high meed. Dying together was one kind of communion. He thought he understood them. He sorrowed for them. How could any love or beauty live in Tordoch? Only weeds could survive, like the flat ugly dockens in the Weavers Lane.

He knew his meditation proceeded on the assumption that the local talk of a suicide pact was the truth. But he knew he couldn't be sure about that. He longed to speak to Rose, to encourage her to live, whatever had happened. It was unthinkable that nobody should ever break the curse of Tordoch and grow up to a proper life. And who more deserving salvation than Rose?

An alcoholic whim took him back to Tordoch between two pubs one night. There was a decent interval since Martha's death. If Rose came along the meeting would seem accidental and he could talk to her of Martha without appearing ghoulish. He slipped into the scheme through the Weavers Lane. On the wall of Donaldson's paint-works he saw REAL COGS RULE ALL, on the back of McLaren's garage was COGLAND, and leaving the lane he saw COGS RULE HERE chalked on Kennedy's soap-factory.

He loitered in a closemouth. It was raining. It had been raining all day. Across the dark street the windows of a fish-and-chip shop and a general-stores stared through the downpour with a flood of inane brilliance. He would see Rose silhouetted there if she passed. He would know her walk and figure at once. He waited and waited, wearing an old coat and a waterproof cap as his disguise.

A big puddle in the gutter reflected the building opposite him, making it plunge into the ground as much as it reared above it. He knew it was madness. There was no reason why she could come. He knew she lived just round the corner. That's why he was waiting where he was. But where would she be going or coming from at that time of night with the rain lashing down? His feet were cold. He felt the damp seep into his bones. He gave it up and went back to his pubcrawl.

The papers had an epilogue to their story of the young lovers. Roy's parents had no comment. But there was an interview with Martha's father plus his picture. He wanted to make a statement he said. He had a grievance. People were saying his daughter was pregnant when she died. He and his wife wanted to have it publicly declared there was no truth in the rumour. After that there was nothing more in the papers, and the Weipers moved quietly from Tordoch two months later.

Mr Alfred too let it drop out of mind. He was having worries of his own. Before the session ended he was transferred to a primary school. Mr Charles Parsons, M.A. (Hons.), B.Sc., Ed.B., FEIS, saw him out with a smile and a handshake.

'I should very much have liked to have kept you here. But you understand you were only standing in for Mr Auld till he recovered from his operation. Now he's back I've no timetable for you. It's a pity. But I'm sure you'll enjoy teaching in Winchgate Primary. It's a fine modern school. It was only opened a year ago.'

'Oh yes,' said Mr Alfred.

He knew he had lost face at Waterholm, but he had never expected to be sent to a primary school.

'You've always taught post-primary, haven't you?' Mr Parsons asked as if he didn't know.

'Yes,' said Mr Alfred. 'I've been teaching secondary classes for —'

'Then this will be a challenge to you,' said Mr Parsons. He was smooth and quick. He didn't want Mr Alfred talking back. 'I always say teaching is a job that's full of new challenges. One must accept the challenge.'

'Yes, I know,'said Mr Alfred. 'But I —'

'Children are delightful to teach at that age,' said Mr Parsons. 'So innocent, so keen to learn. I've taught primary classes myself, you know. I'd love to get back into the classroom and do some solid teaching, instead of all this admin. I'm sure you as a graduate will find it most rewarding to work with primary children.'

'Yes, I'm sure,' said Mr Alfred.

TWENTYSIX

When he got to Winchgate Primary he was told his class was in an annexe a mile from the main building.

Mr Chambers, the headmaster, received him in a pleasant office with picture-windows, central-heating, a fitted carpet, a modern desk with matching chair, glass-fronted bookcases, a coffee table and a jar of mixed flowers. He had two phones on his desk, a master-radio and an intercom panel behind him, and four lounge-chairs for his visitors.

Mr Lauder, the deputy head, hovered respectfully. Mr Alfred recognised him as a type rather than an individual. A deferential man, useful to his superiors, discreet and stonefaced, conspiratorial if need be, and all the time taking care of his own interests. Never without a paper in his hand to make him look busy.

'I'm sorry I've got to put you in the annexe,' said Mr Chambers, smiling broadly. 'But I can't send an established member of staff down there to make room for you here. You'll have to sort of thole your assizes in the outposts of empire till there's a vacancy in the main building. It's the curse of a primary school, an annexe.'

'There's hardly a primary school without one now,' said Mr Lauder.

He raised sad eyes from a sheaf of foolscap held by a bulldog-clip.

'Some have two,' said Mr Chambers. 'Sandy Logan over in Clachanwood, he has three, poor man.'

'He must be getting on now, old Sandy,' said Mr Lauder. 'He's about due to retire I should think. And did you see wee Jimmy Rae died yesterday?'

'Yes, I saw it in the *Herald*,' said Mr Chambers. 'All that superannuation and he never lived to draw a penny of it.'

'That means a new head wanted for his place,' said Mr Lauder. 'There's bound to be a call-up soon. There's only two left on the reserve list.'

'You'd better get busy,' said Mr Chambers. 'If you want your own school.'

'There's nothing I can do,' said Mr Lauder. 'I don't know anybody.'

He lowered his head, darted a tick at the top sheet of his clip and turned it over.

Mr Alfred waited silently.

'Ah yes,' said Mr Chambers. 'Well, yes, now.'

'Yes,' said Mr Alfred.

The annexe he was sent to was a row of six classrooms in prefabricated huts. They were shoved up thirty years ago as temporary accommodation to take the overflow from the old school till the new one was built, and they were still needed because the new school was too small even before it was opened. They were drab lairs with hardboard walls and wooden floors. At the end of the row was a cell used as a staffroom. It had a deal table and no tablecloth, five hard chairs, a gas-ring and a two-bar electric fire, a tiny toilet round the corner and a wash-hand basin with no hot water. Mr Alfred sighed and tightened his jaws till his decadent molars ached again.

He was uneasy in his new job. He had no idea how to talk to children ten years old. They might have been ten months old for all he knew about people so young. They seemed babies, and like Mr Briggs he thought there were already too many babies in the world. He had never had boys and girls in the same room before. He had never had forty-eight pupils in the same room before. He had never worked through the day without a change of class or a period off before.

'You'll be all right here,' said Mr Lindsay, senior resident and cynic, an older man. 'Nobody bothers us. Up in the main building you've always got the boss breathing down your neck. I prefer it down here. I don't like these new schools they're putting up. This is what I'm used to. That's why I volunteered to stay here. You can be independent. Nothing to worry about. Old Chamber-pot, he won't put any class in the annexe for more than six months. So they come and they go and I stay. Suits me. Never see wee Lauder either. Can't stand that man. That's why I asked out of the main building. And they can't pin a thing on you when you've had the class less than six months. You'll like it here, an old hand like you.'

Mr Alfred didn't like it. He wanted to teach. But nobody wanted to learn. He knew it was his job to make them. He tried. He failed. It was like talking into a phone with nobody at the other end. His troubled conscience found a line of defence. He took the progress cards for every pupil in his own class, in Mr Lindsay's class, and in two other classes. He listed the intelligence quotients recorded there and worked out the average. It was ninety-two. The mean was ninety.

'No wonder we can't do much,' he said. 'They just haven't got it. Do you think it's possible there are more stupid children now than there were in our time?'

'Now, now!' said Mr Lindsay.

He raised a censorious finger and grinned. A man as earnest as Mr Alfred amused him.

'What do you mean — now, now?' said Mr Alfred.

'You must never say a child is stupid,' said Mr Lindsay. 'There are no stupid children, just as there are no bad children.'

'But there are,' said Mr Alfred. 'Whether you believe in original sin or believe in evolution, you can't deny there's wickedness and stupidity in the world.'

'You know that and I know that,' said Mr Lindsay. 'But the top brass won't admit it. They've never worked nine till four, Monday to Friday in a classroom. They talk as if there was only a shower of little Newtons and Einsteins who haven't had a fair chance because you didn't teach them right.'

'I see,' said Mr Alfred.

'And if the boy is a thief, a liar and a coward, it's not his fault. It's yours for not giving him enough love.'

'It's a very attractive theory,' said Mr Alfred. He turned it over and looked at it. 'No child is bad. Then all children are not bad. Does that mean good? No child is stupid. All children are not stupid. Does that mean clever?'

'You're so new in primary teaching,' said Mr Lindsay, 'you don't seem to know the line. All children are equal. So why should the clever ones get prizes? Either give them all prizes like in Alice in Wonderland or give nobody a prize. If everybody can't get something it's only fair nobody should get anything. If you deprive a child of a prize you make him feel he's inferior. You might warp him for life. We've got to discourage the competitive spirit. It's a bad thing. So no more exams. Some poor sod might fail.'

Mr Alfred said the new schemes of work, and the new methods they involved, were making life difficult.

'I don't know what I'm trying to do,' he complained.

'Does anybody?' said Mr Lindsay.

'Another thing,' said Mr Alfred. 'It doesn't seem this school was ever meant for teaching in. It's more like a welfare centre. I've never met so many cases of free dinners and free clothes and getting tokens for the clinic. We feed them and clothe them and give them medical care. Next thing is we'll be putting them to bed.'

'Wouldn't be surprised,' said Mr Lindsay. 'Once you start with the idea all children are equal, next thing is you say some of them don't get a fair chance because they come from a poor home. So tomorrow or the day after we'll be having legislation for equal environments. We'll have the mums and dads in barracks and all the weans brought up together in one bloody big comprehensive sleeping-and-feeding-centre.'

'Back to Sparta,' said Mr Alfred.

'It's bound to come,' said Mr Lindsay. 'You can have liberty or you can have equality. You can't have both.'

'What about fraternity?' said Mr Alfred.

'Haven't seen it since I left the army,' said Mr Lindsay.

'No, I suppose not,' said Mr Alfred.

There was a young teacher, Miss Seymour, two doors along the veranda from him, a female non-graduate college-trained for three years. She had been teaching for a year and a bit. He thought her youth and her zest for the job might help him if he discussed the new methods with her. Inadvertently he mentioned poetry.

She boggled.

'Poetry? Oh, I never do poetry. I encourage the children to write their own poetry.'

She was airy-mannered, brisk-moving, swift-speaking, and fully fashionable. She decorated the walls of her classroom with the drawings and paintings of her pupils and pinned up the foolscap pages of a handwritten class-magazine.

Mr Alfred inspected the display, hoping to learn something.

'Wouldn't it be better to let the children see some good reproductions of famous paintings?' he asked. 'Or even coloured posters of Scotland's beauty-spots. You can get them from British Railways.'

'That's no good,' said Miss Seymour. 'It's the children's own work that's important.'

'I see there's a lot of bad spelling and bad grammar in your magazine,' he said.

'Spelling and grammar don't matter,' said Miss Seymour. 'Just so long as they write something. Creative activity, that's what counts.'

'But very few folk are creative,' said Mr Alfred. 'Even those that are need examples when they're young. Shouldn't you let them see a painting by a great painter, let them learn a poem written by a poet? Instead of all this rubbish.'

She laughed at him.

'Rubbish? I like that! You're a right old fossil! What you see there is what the inspectors want. This is the day of the child-dominated classroom.'

'The child is master of the man,' he muttered.

'Pardon?' she said.

She used a pale pink lipstick, her nails were varnished silver, her hair was a long sheeny blonde, she wore fishnet tights and a miniskirt. She had pale-blue eyes, a small nose and a big bosom. But she didn't attract him. Since the day he lost Rose he had become impotent and lost interest in women. He had even forgotten Stella. He never went to her pub now.

'Don't worry so much,' Mr Lindsay patted him on the elbow. 'All this will pass. In education the experts of one generation always discover the experts of the previous generation were a crowd of bloody eedjits.'

'I don't doubt it,' said Mr Alfred. 'But I'm afraid the new fashion will last my time.'

At the lunch-hour break, to get away from it all, he went for a walk round the neighbourhood. There was a new park five minutes away, and he felt the better for a walk round it in spite of the fact that the urinal at the main entrance had GATE YA BASS daubed on the wall and YY GATE chiselled on the door of the solitary water-closet. There were two pubs, but he didn't go into either. He never touched alcohol till his day's work was over. One of the pubs was new, but the other, the Black Bull, was an old howff surviving from the days when Winchgate like Tordoch was only a village on the edge of the insatiable city. There was an old cinema, the Dalriada, dating from the Chaplin era, and behind the park a local railway line closed by Beeching. There was a public library and reading room. And further out, he was told, there was a cemetery beside the old village church. He meant to visit it some lunchtime, but procrastinated. He saw himself trying to make out the inscriptions on the weatherworn tombstones and going over some stanzas of Gray's 'Elegy' in his head. The library too he meant to visit. It would be peaceful there and in the cemetery.

But he found no peace. He got used to the janitor accosting him every Monday morning.

'Another break-in at the week-end, sir. Sorry it's your room again. But you see, it's you being at the far end. They've a clear getaway across the field and over the railway. Even if I spotted them I could never catch them.'

The first time it happened was the worst. He thought it was an attack on him as much as on the room. He thought he must have antagonised his boys somehow. All his windows were smashed and the classroom entered. Textbooks and exercise-books were torn to bits and the scraps scattered. The desks had been pushed about and overturned. The walls were sprayed with paint, and chalk was stamped into the floorboards. The pupils were jubilant when they came in and saw chaos. Mr Alfred tried to settle them and sort things out, but it took a long time.

'Please sir, I still haven't got the right seat.'

'Please sir, I've got books here aren't mine.'

'Please sir, there's dirt in my desk.'

They were excited, curious to see what he would do. Mr Alfred rubbed his chin. He felt the bristles coarse under his fingertips. He never seemed to get a close shave in the morning now. He breathed in and breathed out, slowly.

His windows were broken three weeks running, but when other rooms were raided as well he stopped thinking it was his fault. The fourth week-end Mr Lindsay's room was nearly set on fire. All that was left of the register and the pupils' documents, progress cards, medical schedules and report cards, was a charred mass in a corner where the floorboards and the wall were badly scorched. The invaders put the water-closets out of use by stealing the chains that flushed the cisterns. The janitor tied cords to the lever in lieu of chains, but they soon disappeared too. The ceiling in the toilets had big holes caused by boys swinging from the lintel of the cubicle-doors to see how high and hard they could kick. The damage was so recurrent repairs became desultory.

'I'm sick of this place,' said the janitor.

He was an old-fashioned man, impatient of children, much given to whining about the hard life he had. He spent his days moaning in the huts and his nights drinking in the Black Bull. He was there one night when his lonely wife heard glass breaking. She hurried out just in time to see three lads scampering. She was angry, and in her anger she spoke foolishly.

'I know you,' she called out in the twilight. 'I know you, McCulloch! I saw you, Baxter! Yes, and you with the red hair, I know you too!'

She told her husband. He challenged McCulloch and Baxter in the morning. He thought he would get the third boy's name by threatening them. All he got was abuse. When it was dark that night somebody threw a brick through his living-room window. At the end of the month he handed in his resignation.

'I'm not putting up with this any longer,' he told Mr Alfred. 'I'm getting a job with the Parks Department.'

He wasn't there a week before he was moaning again. Mr Alfred met him on one of his lunchtime walks.

'I've just lost eight young trees,' said the ex-janitor. 'They must have come prepared to do damage. It would have took a good axe to fell they trees. It would break your heart, so it would.'

'Oh dear,' said Mr Alfred. 'I don't understand it.'

To avoid having to listen to the ex-janitor's grumbling he stopped going to the park. He went further out to have a look at the cemetery he had long meant to visit. It was a restful plot, away from the world and divorced from time, but before he was very far in he saw two tombstones lying flat. A wizened labourer was bent on putting them up again. He straightened when he heard Mr Alfred come along. He had to tell somebody.

'But how did they manage it?' said Mr Alfred.

'They broke into my toolshed,' said the old man. 'It took a crowbar to get these stones down. I give up. Folk that'll do that, they've no respect for nothing.'

'Oh dear,' said Mr Alfred. 'I can't understand it.'

He was in low spirits at that time in any case, because Granny Lyons was in hospital. She was to have a mammectomy. He went out at midday to phone the hospital and ask about her. He didn't like to use the phone in the school in case he was overheard. He preferred to keep his private life private. He walked round and round Winchgate for an hour and got nowhere. Every phone-box he tried was out of order.

'Oh dear,' he said. 'I'll never understand it.'

Still searching peace and quiet he went next day to the local library. He liked going to the corporation's public libraries, he liked showing his spare ticket to get in, and then browsing through the catalogues and the card-index of recent additions. The librarian on duty that day was a sedate little spinster with grey hair and a cameo brooch on her blouse. When she saw Mr Alfred come in she knew at once he was a booklover. She watched him go to where the catalogues should be, watched him squint for the card-index boxes. She sighed, padded over in flatheeled sympathy. She explained the library had no catalogues. There had been a break-in through the skylight. All the index-cards and the printed catalogues had been stolen. Some of the cards had been found scattered across the old railway line, but she couldn't say yet how many were missing. The printed catalogues, bound in volumes, had still to be found.

'We'll have to recatalogue the whole library,' she said.

'Oh dear,' said Mr Alfred. 'What a shame.'

She blinked and sniffed, acknowledging his share in her sorrow.

'Fourteen thousand volumes,' she said. 'I don't know how long it will take us. We're short of staff as it is.'

'Oh dear,' said Mr Alfred. 'I don't understand. Why do they do it?'

He was glad he wasn't a cinema-goer when he saw from the bus one morning that the Dalriada was only the hollow shell of a burned-out building. But he wasn't surprised. He knew he was in a bad area. He seemed to have spent his life in bad areas. And he supposed the annexe where he taught was the prey of vandals because it was a neglected backwater lacking the amenities of the main building. It bred resentment, and resentment was expressed in destruction. That's how he explained it to Mr Lindsay.

Mr Lindsay smiled. He knew the main building was having trouble too. The climax came when a single-storeyed wing was gutted by fire. A passing motorist saw the flames at two in the morning. The wing included a dining-room, kitchen, gymnasium, and medical room. The papers said it cost more than £100,000 when it was opened. The police said entry had been gained through a pantry-window too small to admit anyone but a schoolchild. Mr Chambers had to make emergency arrangements to feed the children who used the dining-room their schoolmates had destroyed.

'I can just see old Chamber-pot,' said Mr Lindsay. 'Chasing his tail in ever decreasing circles till he disappears up his own arse.'

'Oh dear,' said Mr Alfred. 'What a school!'

'Ah now, wait a minute!' said Mr Lindsay, aggressively loyal. 'It's not just here. It happens everywhere.'

'The child-dominated school,' said Mr Alfred.

'That's not a fair thing to say,' said Miss Seymour.

TWENTYSEVEN

Mr Alfred liked the week-end. He could forget school and Miss Seymour then. On a Saturday afternoon he went strolling along Sauchiehall Street. He meant to go to Boots and buy shaving-soap and razor-blades. But he was on the wrong side of the road, and when he came out of a daydream he saw he couldn't get across. Where there should have been four lanes of one-way traffic racing from west to east, with a break at Hope Street or Renfield Street on the Cross signal, there was only a crowd of pedestrians from east and west who kept going on a collision course. He thought it rather strange so many people should be walking right in the middle of a busy road. It took him a moment or two to make out that what he was seeing was two gangs, about fifty in each, armed with axes and hammers, throwing bottles and yelling as they advanced.

He was frightened by the noise and the flourish of weapons. When the rearguards flowed from the road on to the pavement, routing neutrals there, he ran into a shopdoorway. He wasn't the only one. All the shopping housewives flocked for cover, and their hysterical screams made bedlam of a battlefield already bellowing and rebellowing. He saw a scampering matron trip herself in her hurry and fall on her face just as an empty bottle crashed beside her. He was terrified, but he thought he had to be at least a gentleman if not a hero. He dashed from his shelter and tried to help her to her feet. She was fat and heavy. He couldn't lift her. He felt the sag of big flabby breasts as he grasped her round the middle and he blushed. Some women, gabbling indignantly, gave him a hand and raised their fallen sister. She got off her knees slowly, white and shaking.

When he had calmed her a little and taken her to the doorway Mr Alfred turned to watch what was going on in the street. He was still frightened, but he was interested too. He couldn't believe that two gangs had the cheek to pick Sauchiehall Street on a Saturday afternoon as the venue for a challenge match, Sauchiehall Street above all places, the city's most famous thoroughfare, its answer to Edinburgh's Princes Street, to London's Regent Street.

He looked and listened. The medley of chanting and barracking made it hard to distinguish the words, but he recognised the same warcry coming from both sides.

'Ya bass!'

'Ya bass!'

'What's it all about?' he asked in the doorway.

Nobody seemed to know. Nobody even looked at him, far less answered him. All eyes front, all mouths open.

Before the gangs were fully engaged six patrol cars and a Q car came speeding along. They barged through them and swerved to a stop in the middle of the road. A score of policemen jumped out. Mr Alfred wanted to cheer. He saw the crowd break like shattered glass, he saw youths throw away bottles and bayonets as they fled. He saw a butcher's cleaver tossed in the air and heard it clatter in the gutter. A discarded hammer landed at his feet. He gaped at it.

In the Sunday paper he read there were twenty-nine arrests. The printed story pleased him. He had to cut it out. He had to show it to Mr Lindsay in the staffroom on Monday morning.

'I saw that,' he had to say. 'I was there.'

The cutting seemed to give more reality to what he had seen, and what he had seen made the cutting more credible.

He saw another fight in the street before he was much older. Mr Lindsay, a judicious beer-drinker, told him of a bar in the south-side that served good draught beer. Mr Alfred said he would give it a trial. A pub-crawl in that area might be interesting. He took a bus across the river on a Wednesday night. He thought Wednesday would be a suitably quiet night for a voyage of exploration and he got off the bus with the pleasant feeling of a day's work behind him and adventure in front of him.

Between pubs he walked into trouble. Two companies of juveniles, moving against each other at the gallop, took over the whole street and made anybody who got in their way scurry into a close for safety. Mr Alfred resented having his hard-earned right to a pub-crawl obstructed. He had a drink in him, and he wasn't going to run into a close just because of a clash of minors. He stood against a shop-window and superciliously looked on. What he saw alarmed him and wiped the sneer off his face. The vicious way the fangs were bared at the scream of 'Ya bass' seemed an appalling and yet appropriate accompaniment to the thrust of the knife.

Squad cars and a dog-van bowled along and closed in as the battle rolled along Victoria Road and into Calder Street. The dogs were taken from the van but not released in pursuit. Their barking was enough to make the rioters run.

The next morning he saw in his paper there were fourteen arrests. He read it out to Mr Lindsay. Again he had to boast.

'I saw that. I was there.'

'But you found my pub all right?' said Mr Lindsay.

'Oh yes,' said Mr Alfred. 'You're quite right. It's a good beer they have there. But you know what I'm finding now? It's hard to get a good light draught beer. It's mostly heavy ale they serve now. That's what the young ones ask for. They just want to get drunk quick. You can see it. Two pints and they want to fight their pal.'

The frequency of gang-fights in the main streets of their city became a staple of conversation between them. They told each other what they had seen in town the night before, they read aloud from the paper over their cup of tea at morning-break.

'Policeman stabbed in gang-affray,' read Mr Lindsay.

'Five stabbed on way to dance,' read Mr Alfred.

'Boy of sixteen gets six years,' read Mr Lindsay. 'Attempted murder by stabbing.'

'Boy of seventeen gets four years,' read Mr Alfred. 'Used razor on a girl and a youth in gang-clash.'

Minor disorders they noted too.

'Shots hit buses on terror route,' read Mr Lindsay.

'Bus rowdy jailed for thirty days,' read Mr Alfred.

'Nine arrests after dance brawl,' read Mr Lindsay. 'A gang of youths entered a dance-hall shouting, We are the little people! We've come to rule the world.'

'I like that,' said Mr Alfred. 'The little people.'

'Come to rule the world,' said Mr Lindsay.

'Surely the Second Coming is at hand,' said Mr Alfred.

'That's Yeats, isn't it?' said Mr Lindsay. 'The Second Coming. It's a poem by Yeats. Am I right?'

'Yes, you're quite right,' said Mr Alfred. 'The blood-dimmed tide is loosed. The ceremony of innocence is drowned.'

'Oh, I don't remember that,' said Mr Lindsay. 'But I know I've seen a poem by Yeats called the Second Coming.'

Mr Alfred was surprised a fellow-teacher in a primary school had read Yeats. He began to like Mr Lindsay.

TWENTYEIGHT

It was payday again. He was glad. He kept out of debt, but he had no savings. By the time the end of the month came round he was beginning to need money. He had his cheque in his hand by ten o'clock and cashed it locally before lunch. Money was all the armour he took on his nightly tour of dark streets and dingy pubs, in search of a castle perilous and a holy grail.

Sometimes, as he wandered, there lurked in a forgotten corridor of his mind a twin accusing him that for all his boasted love of literature he hadn't read a book right through for a long time, that the most modern poets he had read were those in fashion thirty years ago, that he had stopped there and never read anyone younger than himself.

At those moments he felt his cloak of booklover was as shabby as the old coat he was wearing. He wished he had a quiet corner where he could sit in some comfort at a big desk and resume the studies of his youth. He blamed his truancy on the lack of a house of his own. His lodgings were so cramped he could use them only as a den for eating and sleeping, and even at that he often ate out. But over the years he had put off from day to day the attempt to find a better place. Where he was had one advantage he valued. It allowed him a wide liberty of coming and going as he pleased. To move might limit his freedom and would certainly mean a new routine. The prospect didn't please him. He was a creature of habit.

'And this is a bad habit,' he said to his silent face in a bar mirror. 'This paynight binge.'

When he had a month's salary in his pocket he always drank more than usual. The way the world looked then was part of the colour of paynight. So leaving the last pub when the bell went he knew he had enough, if not too much. Out in the street he was aware of being hungry as well as drunk.

'No, not drunk,' he said, encouraging himself to get past people without colliding. 'I won't have that. Just a bit fuddled, that's all. What I say is, anaesthetised.'

He passed a new cafeteria with broad uncurtained windows. He saw it was packed with young people shoving a latenight snack down their gullets. The sight of so much esuriency recalled to him a practice of the days when he was only an apprentice in drinking. After a night in a pub he used to go to a cheap restaurant and eat a big plate of fish and chips. His journeyman's stomach seemed to have lost the capacity for that amount of food at that time of night. For years he had gone to bed without a bite after drinking. But now a youthful craving moved in his belly and he aimed at the Caballero for something to eat.

He didn't forget he had a month's pay in his pocket, and he had taken care as usual never to be seen fumbling with a wad of notes when he paid for a drink. He always kept a few pounds loose for easy access, but the bulk of his money he kept stowed away in a pocket inside the waistband of his trousers. It was a pocket he told the tailor to put in whenever he had a new suit. He had never lost any money, never been dipped. He took great pride in that.

Outside the Caballero he made sure he had two notes handy and some loose silver. Groping to count the coins by touch alone, his fingers met a thick cylinder. For a moment he didn't know what it was. Then he remembered it was the felt-tipped pen he had taken from a boy he caught writing GATE YA BASS on the flyleaf of an atlas. He had put the pen in his pocket and forgotten about it. He slipped it aside and went on trying to add up the money in his pocket. He calculated he had enough silver to pay for anything the Caballero could offer, but he was pleased to feel notes there as well. Rather than put out in small change the exact sum required, especially when he wasn't sober, he was much given to handing over a note for each new payment and ending up with a dead weight of silver every night.

The city was full of new eating-places open late, Italian, Indian, Chinese. Keen to compete, the Caballero had modernised its front and furnishings, though not its menus, since he last ate in it. The unfamiliar entrance offended him. The strength needed to push open a heavy glass door threw him off balance and he couldn't get in without a stumble and a stagger. His clumsiness annoyed him. In the abrupt brightness his eyes were slow to focus, and he took conspicuously long to spot a table to suit him. There was one four yards from him, at fortyfive degrees to his angle of incidence, but he missed it.

He loitered two steps inside the door, making a survey that was difficult for him because he was suffering from an unexpected diplopia. He blinked. Right where he was dithering a young man and his girlfriend were eating sausage, eggs and chips baptised with HP sauce. The young man was quick-eyed and kind-hearted. He wanted to show his girlfriend he was a gentleman. He put down his knife. With his right hand freed he tapped Mr Alfred's elbow and thumbed to the vacant table. He looked up. Mr Alfred looked down. The young man smiled. His girlfriend was pleased with him. Mr Alfred bowed to both smiles.

'Thank you,' he said, age respecting youth.

He heard a thickening in his speech and began to feel self-conscious. He advanced obliquely, swimming against the current of departing customers, anxious to reach the undulating table before he drowned.

The young man and his girlfriend weren't the only ones who noticed him come in. A quartet in the back corner stared, watching him all the way till he sat down. Two of the four recognised him.

'That's big Alfy,' said Gerald Provan.

'Christ so it is,' said Smudge.

'Who's big Alfy?' said Dianne McElhimmeny.

'He looks squiffed,' said Yvonne McGudgeon.

'Well away,' said Dianne. 'Who is he?'

'Yous know him?' said Yvonne.

Gerald told them big Alfy used to be his teacher.

'See! See teachers?' said Yvonne. 'Can't stand them so I can't.'

'I hated school so I did,' said Dianne.

'Imagine him coming to a place like this,' said Smudge.

'A man his age,' said Gerald. 'With what he gets paid.'

'He looks a right tramp,' said Yvonne.

'Is he one of yon?' said Dianne. 'You know what I mean.'

'A query?' said Yvonne.

'Nut hom,' said Gerald.

He told them about Rose Weipers.

'Dirty old man,' said Dianne.

'Bad wee bitch that one was,' said Yvonne. 'Letting a drip like that feel her for a couple of bob.'

'I bet you he's loaded,' said Smudge.

'Of course he's loaded,' said Dianne. 'You can see it in his eyes.'

'Not drink, money,' said Smudge.

'Christ you're right, pal,' said Gerald. 'The enda the month the day. The big bugger'll have his pay in his pocket. How about rolling him?'

'That's what I mean,' said Smudge. 'You on, chookies?'

'Wadyathink, Dianne?' said Yvonne.

'Fits okay with you sokay with me,' said Dianne.

They plotted while they waited for Mr Alfred to finish his two hamburgers and coffee. They paid after he paid, stalled a moment more, and followed him out. The girls accosted him on the pavement.

'You a teacher?'said Dianne pleasantly.

Mr Alfred was wary. He always distrusted people who stopped him in the street, especially youths who asked familiar questions.

'Gotta fag, mister?'

'Gotta light, mac?'

'Got the right time, Jimmy?'

The questions were often put to him on his way home at midnight. He didn't like them. He never liked strangers who tried to speak to him as if they were old friends. He thought it was obvious he wasn't a man to be spoken to without an introduction. In his opinion youths who asked a man his age for a cigarette or a match, or even the time, were much too egalitarian in their manners, even in a city famous for its democratic way of life, or else they were rascals. He believed if he looked at his watch to tell them the time they would find out what they wanted to know, that he had a watch. Then they would attack him and take it from him. Or if he stopped to take out a box of matches or a packet of cigarettes he would be off guard for just as long as that took, which would be long enough for them to surround him, and rob him. So he never stopped to answer a question.

But this was different. He was warmed to have two lissom lassies, one at each elbow, hanging on to him and flashing a smile. An old desire stretched in him, so long quiescent it had the thrill of novelty. He couldn't tell a lie. He had to be chatty to girls so friendly, young and pretty. He had to be gallant. He was. They smiled to his smile.

'And was you ever at Collinsburn?' said Yvonne.

'Yes, indeed I was,' he said, and lurched with good will between the pair of them. 'But I'm sorry I don't remember either of you. Of course I didn't have many girls' classes.'

He felt sure he had said clashes. He laughed to laugh it off.

'Aw, you'll no remember me,' said Yvonne.

'Nur me,' said Dianne.

'We was at Collinsburn,' said Yvonne. 'But no in your class.'

'Naw, we never got you,' said Dianne. 'Wasn't we unlucky!'

She laughed. He laughed. They all laughed.

Yvonne squeezed Mr Alfred on one arm, Dianne squeezed him on the other. They hung on tight. They made conversation as instructed. They diverted him.

'But ma wee sister knew you,' said Dianne. 'She was in your class.'

'Oh yes?' said Mr Alfred.

The press of the girls' hands on his arms, the feel of their hips against him, the brush of their lips at his cheek as they chattered, so soothed and yet aroused him that he didn't see he was being led astray from the main road into an empty sidestreet of old tenements.

'So was mines,' said Yvonne.

'Mine,' said Mr Alfred.

'Same class as Rose Weipers,' said Dianne.

'Dyever see wee Rose now?' said Yvonne.

'She's no so wee,' said Dianne. 'You should see the boys that's after her.'

The thought of boys after Rose made Mr Alfred jealous. He suffered.

'Rose?' he said. 'Do you two know Rose?'

'Sure,' said Yvonne.

'Of course,' said Dianne.

'Does she ever,' said Mr Alfred.

He didn't get a chance to say 'mention my name'. Gerald and Smudge came up behind him and bundled him into a close. They acted quickly and efficiently. Gerald was tall and strong, Smudge was smaller but broad and tough in his teens. Yvonne and Dianne let it go with a muted cry as if they were as surprised as Mr Alfred. They watched at the closemouth while Gerald and Smudge roughed him. His head was forced down, their knees and fists were on him. They shoved him smartly into the back-close where they wouldn't be seen from the street and went to work on him. They rifled him when they had him flat and got his loose silver and the two pound notes he kept handy. But they missed the rest of his salary hidden in the waistband of his trousers.

'Was sure he'd've had more,' Gerald panted.

Mr Alfred lay groaning and writhing. He whimpered. He was in pain. The way they had cracked his head against the wall to make him give in left him seeing flashes of lightning in a granular darkness.

'Bastard banks it quick maybe,' said Smudge. 'They toffs. Pay by cheque all the time. Fly.'

'Coo-ee,' called Yvonne.

Gerald kicked Mr Alfred again and spat on him.

'Quick,' said Smudge. 'Somebody coming.'

'He must have more somewhere,' said Gerald.

'Coo-ee,' called Dianne. 'Coo-ee.'

'Ach, leave him,' said Smudge.

He pulled Gerald away from starting another search and they joined the ladies. They returned deviously to the main road and took the first bus that came. They didn't care where it was going. In a shop doorway far from the Caballero they shared the winnings.

'Thought you said he was loaded,' Yvonne complained at the pittance allotted her.

'Ach, shut your face,' said Smudge. 'Wadyedo to earn it anyway?'

'Was us took him,' said Dianne.

'Wayamoanin aboot noo?' said Gerald.

'A'm no moanin,' said Yvonne.

'Well don't then,' said Smudge.

'Was worth it,' said Gerald. 'Just to get that big bastard. Money's not everything, you know.'

Mr Alfred stopped groaning and writhing, stopped whimpering. He lay still in the back-close of the tenement where they left him. Fatigue and alcohol and the crack on the skull and the beating and the kicking were too much for him. He gave in. He was unconscious.

His twin stood over him saying, 'I told you so. You asked for it. Going about the way you do.'

He waited in a dream to be rescued from a nightmare.

TWENTYNINE

Someone shook him, but not roughly, whispered.

'Are you all right, old man?'

The voice was gentle.

Mr Alfred moaned coming round, hearing it lean over him.

'Oh, you poor old soul! How are you feeling?'

The speaker was not yet distinguished. He helped Mr Alfred up, brushed him down with judicious hands, gave him his pubcrawling cap, tidied his coatcollar, straightened his tie for him, patted his cheeks, put him against the wall.

At every touch he exuded sympathy.

'Not know me?' said the faraway voice.

'No,' said Mr Alfred.

He couldn't see yet, only hear. The close was dim. Everything was dim. He wasn't sure he was where he seemed to be. His mind seemed someone else's. So did his feet when he felt himself teetering on them.

The speaker came closer. There was a slight halation of his face, but Mr Alfred could see white teeth smile. The blurred lips moved in friendly speech.

'You used to teach me. Not remember?'

'Your face I think,' said Mr Alfred. 'But your name I don't know.'

'Tod,' said the speaker. 'Not remember?'

The gentle voice changed to harsh. The speaker was hurt not to be remembered.

'No,' said Mr Alfred. 'No, I'm afraid I don't.'

He apologised. He was afraid not to. It seemed to be a youth was talking to him, and youths he knew were dangerous. They had to be spoken to respectfully.

'Do forgive me please. I didn't mean to snub you. Oh no, you mustn't think that. But see it from my side.'

The young face turned into darkness, not bothering to listen. But Mr Alfred had to explain.

'When I taught in Collinsburn I had say forty boys in a class, say three classes on my timetable every session. That's a hundred and twenty boys a year. That's one thousand two hundred in ten years. Not to mention girls. I had a class of girls once. It's too many to expect any man to remember. Two thousand four hundred boys in twenty years. Plus girls.'

Tod came into the light again.

'Good at the old mental, eh?' he said. 'I thought you was an English teacher.'

'A teacher of English,' said Mr Alfred. 'I myself am not English. But even a teacher of English can do a little arithmetic.'

'Funny old man, aren't you?' said Tod. 'I've been

watching you. You've got some weird ideas, so you have.'

The voice changed again. It delivered a sneer. It became aggressive. The illumined face of the speaker moved against the unseen face of the listener.

'For the eye sees not itself,' said Mr Alfred, 'but by reflection. Excuse me. I'm too tired to reflect.'

'I know all about you,' said Tod. 'I know what you are all right. I know what you've been up to.'

Mr Alfred sagged with guilt. He waited to be accused of corrupting Rose Weipers.

But Rose wasn't mentioned.

By an abrupt transition, without hanging about for transport, he was in the house where Tod lived. It was a place he had heard of but never seen, a three-roomed house on the first floor of an abandoned tenement, condemned as unsafe, where teenagers of both sexes who had left home lived rough and slept together on the bare boards. It was called The Flat.

Tod pushed him against the kitchen-sink.

'Think you're the great poet, eh?' he said. 'It's not you, it's me. I'm the one that's the poet.'

'Have you published anything?' Mr Alfred enquired. 'That's the test.'

'Of course I've published something,' said Tod.

'Where?' said Mr Alfred.

'Everywhere,' said Tod.

'What do you mean, everywhere?' said Mr Alfred. 'That's a damn silly answer.'

'Manners,' said Tod. 'You're not talking to one of your pupils now, you know. You're talking to me. Tod.'

'I'm sorry,' said Mr Alfred.

'Tell me this,' said Tod.

He sat at the derelict kitchen-table, elbow on the board, a fingertip on his temple. He made it clear he was thinking.

'Tell you what?' said Mr Alfred.

'What have you with all your education ever wrote to compare with Ya Bass?'

'Your Ya Bass?' said Mr Alfred. 'You mean you wrote Ya Bass?'

'It was me thought it up,' said Tod. 'Me and nobody else. All my own work. Alone I done it.'

'Did,' said Mr Alfred. 'Coriolanus.'

'Did,' said Tod. 'An act of poetic creation so it was. Don't you agree?'

'Yes, indeed,' said Mr Alfred.

Tod stood behind the kitchen-table, hands pulling lapels, and lectured.

'The careful student will appreciate the vowel music and consonantal vigour of these remarkable words. He will hear the sublime derision of the street-urchin's *Yah,* a primitive ideophone, modulated into the polite plural *You,* pronounced *Ya* in the dialect of our northern poet. This striking economy of address is immediately followed by the masterly brevity of *Bass,* a monosyllable with more vehemence and malevolence than the full form *Bastard,* found in the work of the more cultured poets who wrote in the southern dialect. Only someone with a great poetic talent could have invented such language in a society as yet hardly civilised. It is from such vulgar eloquence that a great vernacular poetry arises.'

'Very true,' said Mr Alfred. 'Dante. De vulgari . . .'

He was feeling frightened again. He wanted to please the lecturer.

Tod came round the kitchen-table.

'I'm glad you like Ya Bass,' he said. 'It's my best poem so far. But I've a lot more coming up.'

'I'm sure I'll like them all,' said Mr Alfred.

'You'd better,' said Tod.

'Yes, I know,' said Mr Alfred.

Tod smiled. He was pleased.

'You used to take notes wherever you saw Ya Bass, didn't you?'

'That's right,' said Mr Alfred.

'And you cut bits out the paper about all the fights I fixed, didn't you?'

'That's right,' said Mr Alfred.

'Ah, you're a great man,' said Tod. 'A real documentarian.'

'Docs, ya bass,' said Mr Alfred.

'It was just the last two words I thought up,' said Tod. 'I left the rest to the lads themselves. It only needed a few of them to start it off.'

'Then the sheep,' said Mr Alfred.

'That's right,' said Tod. 'I know mine and mine know me. It gave me variety in uniformity.'

'Unity in diversity,' said Mr Alfred.

'All the same only different,' said Tod.

'The formula is *x*YB,' said Mr Alfred. 'Where YB is a constant and *x* has an infinite number of values.'

'And *x*YB equals CR,' said Tod. 'Where CR is a Cultural Revolution.'

'Yes, indeed,' said Mr Alfred.

'Well, the start of one anyway,' said Tod. 'And if I've got Cogs fighting Fangs and screaming Ya Bass at each other it's all in a good cause surely.'

'What cause?' said Mr Alfred.

'Disorder,' said Tod. 'You can't have a revolution without disorder, now can you?'

'No, I suppose not,' said Mr Alfred.

'What we want,' said Tod, 'is liberty. And there's no liberty in order. And you just think for a minute. The wars of religion were fought with men screaming Ya Bass at each other. In their own language of course. The same with the wars of nationalism. All I've did is reduce human conflict to its simplest terms. My boys from the north get killed fighting my boys from the south? So what? Dulce et decorum est pro housing-scheme mori.'

'The territorial imperative,' said Mr Alfred. 'All you've done, you mean, not all you've did.'

'I'll do more before I'm finished,' said Tod. 'I'm young enough yet. Who's going to stop me? Mind you, I'm proud of what I've did so far.'

'What you've done,' said Mr Alfred. 'You have every

reason to be.'

'Those intellectuals,' said Tod. 'Small fry. They misunderstood me. They wrote Brecht Ya Bass and Beckett Ya Bass. I didn't mean it that way at all. Some folk thought it meant Brecht and Beckett were bastards in my opinion. I never meant no such thing.'

'Oh no, I'm sure you didn't,' said Mr Alfred.

'I've nothing against Brecht or Beckett,' said Tod. 'Or any of the big guys. They have their place in literature and I have mines.'

'Mine,' said Mr Alfred. 'Indeed you have.'

'Another thing,' said Tod. 'The intellectuals, they only wrote it once in the one place. That was no use. They missed the whole point of the operation. I wanted Ya Bass to be ubiquitous. Like those bloody young Cratchits in that thing you read to us the week before Christmas one year. I still remember that, you know.'

'Oh, it's ubiquitous all right,' said Mr Alfred.

'Thanks to me,' said Tod. 'These things isn't accidental. It was me made it ubiquitous. Poets are the unacknowledged legislators of the world. Wordsworth.'

'Shelley,' said Mr Alfred.

'Pedantic old bastard, aren't you?' said Tod.

'I'm sorry,' said Mr Alfred.

'I'm a teacher as well as you only better,' said Tod. 'I gave a course of lectures to a few of the lads. I told them what to do. Where to do it, like. I don't mean just writing on walls everywhere. That was only the basic training. No, I mean action. I got Action Groups going. You know, like revolutionary cells. Three principles. Deride, deface, destroy. It was me suggested scattering the catalogues from a library for example. You saw that one yourself. And it was a good one, wasn't it?'

'Yes, that was a very good one,' said Mr Alfred.

'My lads,' said Tod. 'They're all nice fellows. When you get to know them. Maybe not so bright some of them. But you can teach them. You can organise them. That's what I done. I put it to them.'

He went behind the kitchen-table again, arms waving, voice raised, and put it to them.

'Do you want to be nobody or somebody?'

'Somebody,' said Mr Alfred.

'Do you want to be pushed around or do the pushing?'

'Do the pushing,' said Mr Alfred.

'Do you want to have nothing or do you want to have power?'

'Power,' said Mr Alfred.

'Destroy, destroy, destroy!'

'It's quite safe,' said Mr Alfred. 'Nobody will touch you.'

'The old folks at home will blame themselves.'

'They'll say it's all their fault,' said Mr Alfred.

'It's the fault of society.'

'They must have failed you somehow, somewhere,' said Mr Alfred.

'It's not your fault, lads.'

'On my head be it,' said Mr Alfred.

'About! Seek! Burn! Fire! Kill! Slay!'

'Julius Caesar,' said Mr Alfred.

'You are the little people,' said Tod. 'You are sent to rule the world.'

'I've heard that before,' said Mr Alfred. 'Somewhere. I've forgotten.'

'I'm the new Pied Piper,' said Tod.

'So long as you're new,' said Mr Alfred. 'That's all that matters.'

'It was you taught me,' said Tod. 'Remember? In Hyderabad I freed the Nizam from a monstrous brood of vampire bats. But you know what I done when I went to Hamelin. I'll do the same here. Lead all the weans away from you.'

'I'm sure you will,' said Mr Alfred. 'What you did.'

'Don't forget I'm only starting,' said Tod. 'Every revolution is brought about by a determined minority. You take the twelve apostles.'

'Take the Bolsheviks,' said Mr Alfred. 'Lenin and Trotsky.'

'Take John Knox and the Scotch reformers,' said Tod. 'Think what they done to bonny Scotland. Nothing to what I'm doing.'

'I'm sure,' said Mr Alfred. 'What they did.'

'I've got friends,' said Tod. 'Friends in high places. You know that. You've met them. Your bosses. This is a New International, so it is.'

'We've had four already,' said Mr Alfred. 'All failed.'

'Ah, but this is the best yet,' said Tod. 'This one won't fail. From Aberdeen to Vladivostok. From Omsk and Tomsk to Kirkintilloch, you're all on the way out. All you literary bastards. It's the end of the printed word. Everything's a scribble now. The writing's on the wall. I know. I got it put there.'

'Yes, I've seen it,' said Mr Alfred.

'You wait,' said Tod.

'I've no choice,' said Mr Alfred.

'I've got a new campaign coming up,' said Tod. 'I'm starting a League Against War. I'm going to call it LAW.'

'An acronym,' said Mr Alfred. 'Like POISE.'

'I'm working on a monogram for it,' said Tod. 'Something simple the lads can slap up quick wherever there's a blank space.'

'There are still a few left,' said Mr Alfred.

'Even if there's not I can do a palimpsest, can't I?' said Tod. 'LAW everywhere. Suddenly appearing overnight. That'll fox the public, eh? For a while anyway. I'll let out later on what it means.'

'I saw LAW somewhere,' said Mr Alfred. 'A great while since, a long, long time ago.'

'Not so long,' said Tod. 'I tried it out on a couple of my fellows. But they didn't take to it. And I was too busy with Ya Bass to follow up. But I'm getting on to it again now. I'm finished with YY.'

'I never understood that one,' said Mr Alfred. 'Why YY?'

'If the world belongs to the Young,' said Tod, 'then still more it belongs to the Young Young. I get them at school.

Train up a child in the way he should go, and when he is old he will not depart from it.'

'Proverbs,' said Mr Alfred.

'But I'm more interested in my League Against War now,' said Tod.

'I'm glad you're against war,' said Mr Alfred. 'That's always something.'

'I'm against everything,' said Tod. 'To end war you've got to fight. I'll get the yungins to fight against war because the aldyins are past it. You've had the war to end war. It didn't work. I'm going to give you a League Against War, a LAW to end law. Instead of Cogs and Fangs and Tongs and Toi you'll be seeing LAW everywhere you go. I'll have a new wave of destruction in the name of LAW. I'll have LAW YA BASS and LAW OK and YY LAW. The poor public won't know what's going on. They never do till it's done.'

'What good will it do you?' said Mr Alfred.

'I'm not a do-gooder,' said Tod. 'I believe in the dialectic. The unity of opposites. Law is anarchy. That's what I'm after. I'll do it the way I done Ya Bass. Just a scribble here and a scribble there to start with. Nobody'll bother. But it will spread and spread till the whole city's covered with it. That'll be something. The quantity becomes quality. You said that yourself.'

'But not necessarily a good quality,' said Mr Alfred.

'Who said anything about good?' said Tod. 'It's new. That's all that matters. You admitted that a minute ago. And that's how I'll get revenge.'

'Why do you want revenge?' said Mr Alfred.

'Badness is all,' said Tod. 'You made me what I am today, I hope you're satisfied.'

'If they had slapped down Gerald Provan the first time he stepped out of line this would never have happened,' said Mr Alfred.

'But you don't know it was Gerald Provan rolled you,' said Tod. 'You saw nothing, you heard nothing. They came up behind you. You're only guessing. You've got a spite at Gerald Provan. You're aye picking on him.'

'The way they ought to have stopped the young ruffians in Germany,' said Mr Alfred. 'Before Hitler came to power at all. Terrorising decent people in the street. But no. They even said Hitler himself was all right. He just needed sympathy.'

'The Hitlerjugend weren't ruffians,' said Tod. 'They were good lads. They were organised. I could organise my lads like that. As a matter of fact I'm doing something better. Because you can't pin a thing on me. I'll destroy Europe without a war. You wait. You won't get me in a bloody bunker waiting for a bomb. I'll live to laugh.'

'Who do you think you are?' said Mr Alfred. 'A new Schickelgruber?'

'Who?' said Tod.

'Skip it,' said Mr Alfred.

'You talk the slang of the thirties,' said Tod.

'How do you know?' said Mr Alfred. 'You weren't born then.'

'Was I not?' said Tod. 'I was, I am, and I always will be.'

'You think you're God perhaps?' said Mr Alfred.

'No, the other One,' said Tod. 'The Adversary.'

'The devil seeking whom he may deflower,' said Mr Alfred. 'Der Geist der stets verneint.'

'That's me,' said Tod. 'I say No to you and your likes. I'm nibbling away at the roots of your civilisation. I'll bring it down. The felt-pen is mightier than the sword.'

'You've made my city ugly,' said Mr Alfred. 'Apart from all the stabbings and fighting in the street, this writing on the wall everywhere – it's an offence against civilisation.'

'Civilisation means class-distinction,' said Tod. 'To hell with it. Life is more important than civilisation. Life is a comprehensive school. Every child is equal.'

Mr Alfred raised his hand for permission to speak.

'May I say a poem, please?'

'If you like,' said Tod. 'So long as it's not one of yon there was a young lady of things. Can't stand them.'

Mr Alfred elocuted.

'My heart sinks down when I behold the boys and girls go by.'

He stopped.

'I'm sorry,' he said. 'That is all I can remember.'

'You're getting past it, mac, that's your trouble,' said Tod. 'You should be like me. Young, keen, eager. Accept the challenge. Always learning. I've been thinking I might even learn something from China. You know, the Red Guards. They're fairly knocking the old ones. Taking over the trains. Go where they like. Causing alarm and dismay. I must ask the International Secretariat for more information.'

'You really believe you have an international movement?' said Mr Alfred.

'You can see I have,' said Tod. 'Don't you ever read the papers, mac? I can't lose. I've got a fifth column. You know that. What folk say about me and my lads, it's like what you were saying they said about wee Adolf and his lads. They feel rejected. Give them love. Treat them nice and they'll be nice. Treat them nasty and they'll be nasty.'

'It doesn't work out that way,' said Mr Alfred.

'Yes, you know that and I know that,' said Tod. 'But you mustn't ever say it.'

'They made that mistake about Hitler,' said Mr Alfred.

'It wasn't just wee Adolf,' said Tod. 'Don't forget there was Poor Old Joe as well. He was a great pop figure too in his day before folk decided he was as big a bastard as wee Adolf. You'll remember the pair of them were aye having their picture took with a wee lassie in their arms. You know, cuddling her. They were fond of wee girls, just like you.'

'Excuse me,' said Mr Alfred. 'One only, if you don't mind.'

Tod conceded the correction with a placatory bow and resumed his argument.

'They failed to conquer Europe between them because they were too crude. But see me? I'm subtle. They were there to be named. Not me. I'm nowhere.'

'Everywhere,' said Mr Alfred.

'They'll never catch me,' said Tod.

'No, they won't, will they?' said Mr Alfred.

'Those two stupid bastards wanted a State,' said Tod. 'I don't. I don't want a thousand-year Reich. I don't want a New and Higher Form of Civilisation. I don't want to be the Big Führer Brother Secretary-General. I don't want to conquer Europe. I want to destroy it. Destroy its schools and libraries and public telephones. You can fight an army invading your territory. But you can't fight me. I'm not invading you. I'm already inside. And I'm nobody.'

'Everybody,' said Mr Alfred. 'When I look at what you've done to this city!'

'Go thou and do likewise,' said Tod.

He faded rather than went away.

Mr Alfred found himself out of The Flat as abruptly as he had found himself in it. He teetered at the closemouth.

'How are you feeling now?' said the gentle voice.

'I'll be all right,' said Mr Alfred.

'Now are you sure?' said the young man. 'Are you sure you'll manage?'

'I'll manage fine,' said Mr Alfred.

'It gets worse every night,' said the young man.

'Yes, indeed,' said Mr Alfred.

'Will you get a bus all right?' said the young man.

'I can get one round the corner,' said Mr Alfred.

'I'll leave you then,' said the gentle voice. 'I go this way.'

'I go that way,' said Mr Alfred. 'Good night. And thanks very much.'

'No bother,' said the young man. 'Good night then.'

'Good night,' said Mr Alfred.

THIRTY

When Tod left him Mr Alfred wasn't sure where he was. He was with himself but outside himself, as if there were two of him. He looked up at the nightsky like an ancient mariner trying to take his bearings from the stars. But he couldn't see any stars in the narrow vault between the buildings. All he saw was a crescent reflector hanging in the dark void.

'A falcate moon,' he said.

He repeated the words. They seemed to promise the start of a poem, but the promise wasn't kept. He was distracted from the abortive lyric by a fear he had lost his way. When he went round the corner to get a bus there wasn't a bus to be seen. There wasn't even a bus-stop. He tried another corner and wandered into a hinterland of mean streets. He veered, and got into a tangle of lanes and pends. At that point he wasn't just afraid he was lost. He knew he was lost. He was tempted to panic, but the man with him said it didn't matter, there was always a way out.

The coffee and hamburgers he had taken in the Caballero were meant to sober him. But now he felt drunk again, and always he had the idea he wasn't walking alone. Perhaps it was the crack on the head when he was rolled in the close. Perhaps it was his alarm at losing his way. He thought of going back to the close and starting again from there. But he had zigzagged so much he didn't know if he was walking towards the river or away from it, going east or going west. He plodded on and round about and back again, looking for a main road, one man in him trying to hear the tape of a conversation another had recorded.

Yet for all his confusion he remembered his money. He searched every pocket three or four times. But there was no change. They were all empty. He felt he had been insulted rather than robbed. That most of his month's salary was still safe in his hidden pocket was only what he expected. Had it been gone too he would have groaned in agony. It would have meant the end of his little private world of self-esteem, a mockery of his boast that nobody could ever rob him. The loss of a couple of pounds and a handful of silver was no hardship. It was the degradation of being a victim hurt him.

Now he had a problem. Even if he found a bus going his way he had nothing but fivers to pay his fare. It took him some time to see a taxi was the answer. He wasn't much given to taking taxis. But it had to be done. Instead of looking for a bus-route he began to look out for a cruising taxi. Nothing passed.

He tripped at a dark corner and fell on his knees. He got up shakily. He was frightened. But the other man didn't mind in the least.

The tenements he passed looked shabby, the closes looked slummy. Peeling paint, litter, and dim lights. Everything was dim. Dim and dirty. He longed for the sun and a blue sky and a clean city. He searched his pockets again, still unwilling to believe he hadn't even been left his bus-fare. All he found in one pocket was the thick cylinder he had felt before. The felt-pen, he remembered. And a thin cylinder his fingers recognised as a piece of chalk. He was always finding bits of chalk in his pocket.

'Talk and chalk,' he said. 'That's me. Out-of-date. The child is master of the man. New methods. Visual aids. Projects. Research. Doesn't matter half the bastards can't read. Do research just the same. Discover Pythagoras' theorem for themselves. Could you?'

He stumbled. The flagstones of the city's pavements were seldom flush. He reeled.

'Oh no! Not again!' he cried as he lurched, head down, arms out.

But he didn't fall. He straightened just in time and kept going. And more and more sharply as he wandered through the empty night he was aware of being outside himself, watching himself, listening to himself, not owning himself.

He twisted and turned, corner after corner. He prayed for guidance. Suddenly he came round to shops and neon lights. Then there were hoardings on one side and on the other desolate tenements with all the windows broken, a shuttered pub left standing as the stump of a demolished block, and bulldozers parked in the backcourts of vanished closes. There was nobody about. He went on. And everywhere he went he saw it.

The writing on the wall.

The writing on the wall.

Everywhere he went he saw the writing on the wall.

The writing.
The writing.
The writing on the wall.

TONGS YA BASS   GOUCHO   PEG OK
FLEET YA BASS   YY TOI
TOWN OK
HOODS YA BASS   CODY YYS
SHAMROCK LAND
TORCH RULE OK YY HAWKS MONKS YA BASS

On his right in an all-night urinal COGS YA BASS.
On his left as he rocked YY FANGS OK.

Outside again, still no taxis. No buses. No people. Nothing but the writing on the wall. On every phone-box, junction-box and pillar-box, on every shop-front, bus-shelter and hoarding, on every board and paling, on every bridge and coping-stone there was the writing. Scrawled, scribbled, sprayed, daubed. Yellow, red, green, white, black and blue. Six, eight, ten and twelve inch letters. More writing.

REBELS YA BASS   YY GRINGO   TIGERS
BORDER RULE OK
YY TOON   TUSKY
UZZ RULE   YY CUMBIE   GEMY   TOI LAND

Some old inscriptions too he saw in passing, the weather-faded lettering chalked by children in ancient times.

FUCK THE POPE
SHITE
CELTIC 7–1
1690
FUCK KING BILLY   CUNT

But since they seemed as out-of-date as himself he accepted them without complaint.

He saw a bus-stop with a route-number that would suit him. On the metal frame of the windowless shelter there was slapdashed PRIESTY TOON TONGS. PRIESTY he identified as the name of a housing-scheme the bus-crews refused to service on Saturday nights because the passengers either showed a knife when asked for their fare or kicked and butted the conductor when they jumped off without paying. He swayed and grued.

He had an idea. He would phone the Lord Provost, the *Daily Express* and the University Principal, Mrs Trumbell, the Curator of the Art Galleries and the Secretary of State for Scotland, he would even phone the President of the Educational Institute of Scotland. He would lodge a formal protest. He assumed he could speak to them all at once on the same line. He was all set to ask them for a start, 'Do you folk know what's going on?'

But the first phone-box he went to was out of order. The phone was there in its cradle, sleeping peacefully, never to waken. The cord had been ripped away. His brilliant idea left him. He edged out of the box and waited on the pavement for something to happen. The Muse visited him and he recited aloud impromptu under an arc-lamp.

Was it the same in Carthage, Rome,
Babylon and Ephesus?
To hell! I might as well go home,
If only I could get a bus.

He moved on, wearied. He longed to see again what he had seen as a young soldier with the British Army of Liberation, the gilded buildings of Brussels, the Meir in Antwerp, the Dyver in Bruges, any handsome street in any gracious city. He was no countryman. He liked cities. He longed to live in one.

He forgot he was looking for a taxi. He didn't know where he was going. He wasn't going anywhere. He was standing still. He found that piece of chalk in his pocket again. He fumbled for it. Then he remembered the felt-pen. It was a better instrument. He took it out, unscrewed the cap, held it ready for writing. He heard Tod.

'Go thou and do likewise.'

On a wall he wrote. Carefully, a good scribe. In bold block capitals. Four inches high.

MENE MENE TEKEL UPHARSIN

He stepped back and looked at it. He looked at his work and he thought it was good. He walked along the site, looking for another empty space. But not unnoticed. Two policemen in a patrol-car had seen him. The driver stopped at the kerb. With his mate he watched. They both watched. Frowning one. The other smiling.

'The old bastard's drunk,' said King.

'A foreign bugger,' said Quinn. 'What lingo's that?'

'No idea,' said King. 'He's not a Paki, is he?'

'Doesn't look like one,' said Quinn. 'What's he up to now?'

'Go thou and do likewise,' said Mr Alfred.

He wrote on the wall again.

GLASGOW YA BASS

'Ah, now,' said King.

'We can't have that,' said Quinn.

'It's the first time I've seen anybody right in the act,' said King. 'I mean seen him write.'

Mr Alfred turned away from the wall and shouted to the sky the words he had written.

'Glasgow, ya bass!'

He shouted them so loudly he seemed to want to waken the whole sleeping city and make it listen to him. He nodded and nodded, went back to the wall and ticked off the phrase.

'Right,' he said quietly. 'Next, please.'

He held out his left hand for the next pupil's jotter, his felt-pen in his right ready for marking.

'The old scunner,' said Quinn.

'He didn't look the type to me,' said King. 'Too old I'd have thought.'

'That's the trouble,' said Quinn. 'Once it starts, every bloody fool.'

'Go and get him,' said King. 'Before he falls down.'

'Right,' said Quinn.

King sat back and waited.

Quinn eased from the car and crossed over. No hurry.

'Now, now,' he said. 'What do you think you're playing at?'

'Good evening,' said Mr Alfred.

'Now don't try and be funny,' said Quinn. 'Know what time it is?'

'Oh, I'm not being funny,' said Mr Alfred. 'There's nothing funny about it. That's my point. It's not a pantomime joke, not in my opinion.'

'You should be in your bed, old fella,' said Quinn. 'It's after two.'

'Indeed?' said Mr Alfred. 'I wondered why I couldn't get a bus.'

'What are you writing on the wall for?' said Quinn.

Mr Alfred had no answer. He felt wedged in a cleft. The writing on the wall had been done by someone occupying his body in space and time, someone not identical with himself, someone who had suddenly gone away and left him to answer for what had been done. And while he knew he wasn't responsible for all this writing on the wall he knew he had to answer for it. He didn't mind. He was willing to answer for it, if he was pushed. This young policeman could do what he liked with him. Nothing mattered any more. He had done what he was told to do. He remembered an old word cherished in his youth when a dictionary was his bedside book. Ataraxia. The indifference aimed at by the stoics. That was all he felt.

'Come on,' said Quinn. 'You've had too much I think.'

He took Mr Alfred by the elbow, led him to the car. Put him in the back seat. But gently.

Settling well back Mr Alfred muttered away.

'Since that lout defied me. Nothing but. Schools, libraries, parks, railways, buses, cemeteries. Since that day that lump. All vandalised. The child is master. All natural piety gone. Insolence, be thou my courtesy.'

His head lolled. He jolted and came up again.

'Taught them language. And the profit on it is. Caliban shall be his own master. That blonde bitch Seymour. She should say less. What the inspectors want. Do-it-yourself poetry. Matthew Arnold was an inspector too. What would he say now? Culture and anarchy. Anarchy. Every child a poet, every child a painter.'

He shook his head. He felt sleepy. But he wanted to speak.

'Insolence, violence,' he said. 'It's the black-ground of those torrible grousing-schemes.'

'I told you he was drunk,' said King to Quinn.

Mr Alfred leaned over and tapped Quinn on the shoulder.

'Do you know,' he said, 'you can pick up a lunar probe but you can't pick up a phone.'

'You're right there, pop,' said Quinn.

King braked at a red light. Mr Alfred fell back on his seat and talked to himself.

'Standards must be maintained. We must pass on our cultural heritage. The tongue that Shakespeare spoke, that Milton. Though fallen on evil days, on evil days though fallen and evil tongues, in darkness and with dangers compassed round, and solitude.'

'He's got an educated voice,' said King to Quinn.

'He looks a real scruff to me,' said Quinn to King.

Mr Alfred was comfortable in the back seat. It was better than any bus. He thought he was being taken home in a taxi. He wondered how much it would cost. He wondered how they knew where he lived.

Quinn half-turned, speaking over his shoulder.

'What did you want to go and do a daft thing like that for?'

'Wir müssen aussprechen was ist,' said Mr Alfred.

Quinn shrugged back to King.

'I told you he was a foreign bastard,' he said.

'That's German,' said King to Quinn. 'Maybe he's a refugee from the Iron Curtain.'

'Iron curtain my arse,' said Quinn.

King drove humming along the empty road in the small hours.

Peering through the window Mr Alfred saw the writing on the wall again.

'This great warm-hearted friendly city,' he said. 'The dear green place. The corn is green. How green was my valley. A lot of balls.'

'What's that you were saying?' Quinn turned to ask.

'That it could so preposterously be stained,' said Mr Alfred.

Quinn kept turned round.

'Are you all right, pop?' he asked. 'You know, you're in trouble. Defacing property. Drunk and disorderly. A man your age. You ought to know better.'

'We all ought to know better,' said Mr Alfred.

'Eh?' said Quinn.

Mr Alfred said nothing.

'Nothing to say for yourself, eh?' said Quinn.

Mr Alfred remembered something to say. He said it solemnly.

'For nothing this wide universe I call, save thou, my Rose, in it thou art my all.'

Quinn turned back to King.

'Oh Jesus,' he said.

King took a quick glance over his shoulder.

'Steady up, old fella,' he said. 'Get a hold of yourself.'

Mr Alfred fell asleep.

THIRTYONE

Sheriff Stairs wasn't impressed by Mr Alfred. He didn't like the look of him at all. It was bad enough when irresponsible juveniles went about writing on walls, but it was intolerable when the culprit was a grown man, and above all a man in Mr Alfred's position. If he was an alcoholic he shouldn't be teaching. If he was suffering from a nervous breakdown he shouldn't be teaching. If he was a harebrained eccentric he shouldn't be teaching.

Mr Alfred had nothing to say. He had a return of his old feeling that he was the man outside somebody else. There was a man there in the dock with his face, answering to his name, but it wasn't him. It was another man he had been forced to keep company with, a fellow-traveller who was getting by on a borrowed birth-certificate.

Sheriff Stairs had him remanded for a medical report. The doctor found him sound in wind and limb, but noticed a recent prosthodontia which may have accounted for his pyknophrasia when he was arrested. Heart in good condition, no VD, reflexes, blood-count and urine normal, weight about the average for his height and age, a slight presbyopia. He also found evidence of a femoral hernia, and arranged for a surgeon to operate within a fortnight. Until then, he passed him on to Mr Knight, psychiatrist.

Mr Knight was unofficially accompanied by Mr Jubb, a psychiatrist from England. Mr Jubb had published a paper on *Some Common Phobias of Metropolitan Man.* He had come north with letters of introduction in search of material for a supplementary paper. He found nothing in Edinburgh to detain him and cut west across country to more fertile ground. Mr Knight grudgingly let him sit in on his interrogation of Mr Alfred. Mr Jubb called it an interesting case. Duly silent, he sat in a corner with a big looseleaf notebook and a ballpoint.

'Is it because you're not happy in your work you drink so much?' said Mr Knight. 'Don't you like children?'

'Not in bulk,' said Mr Alfred. 'They frighten me.'

Mr Jubb made a note.

'You're out round the pubs every night, aren't you?' said Mr Knight.

'Oh yes, every night practically,' said Mr Alfred.

'No matter what the weather?' said Mr Knight.

'Not in fog,' said Mr Alfred. 'I hate fog.'

Mr Jubb made a note.

'I'm afraid to cross the street then,' said Mr Alfred. 'Indeed. I'm afraid to cross the street at any time these days.'

'You don't seem to have any social life,' said Mr Knight. 'Don't you like meeting people?'

'Can't say I do,' said Mr Alfred. 'I don't take to strangers easily.'

Mr Jubb made a note.

'You prefer to be alone?' said Mr Knight.

'Yes,' said Mr Alfred. 'I have a great horror of crowds.'

Mr Jubb made a note.

'I hate to feel people knocking against me, touching me,' said Mr Alfred.

Mr Jubb made a note.

'You're not afraid of anything happening to you when you wander round like that?' said Mr Knight.

'I've always had a fear of being robbed,' said Mr Alfred. 'But I take care. I've got this pocket, you see.'

He showed it. He wanted to prove he was a wise old man.

Mr Jubb made a note.

'I've never been attacked before,' said Mr Alfred. 'I was terrified. I thought I was going to die.'

Mr Jubb made a note.

Mr Alfred bit the nail of his index finger. He wasn't given to biting his nails. But there was a ragged edge annoying him. He had felt it catch on the cloth when he was showing his secret pocket and he tried to bite it off.

Mr Jubb made a note.

'Not that I should like to live till I'm senile,' said Mr Alfred.

He smiled. Mr Knight didn't. Mr Jubb made a note.

'Did you have much to drink the night you were attacked?' said Mr Knight.

'Not much,' said Mr Alfred. 'Not really. I've had more. Often. Say seven or eight pints and seven or eight whiskies. Maybe more. But then I'm used to it. I remember one night –'

He stopped. He didn't want to tell too much.

Mr Jubb made a note.

'You've no friends apparently,' said Mr Knight. 'But have you no pets? A cat or a dog for example.'

'Oh no, I can't stand animals,' said Mr Alfred.

Mr Jubb made a note.

'Least of all cats,' said Mr Alfred. 'They give me the creeps.'

Mr Jubb made a note.

'Even insects,' said Mr Alfred. 'I loathe spiders.'

He wanted to chat to Mr Knight, to help him. He felt sorry for a man who had to ask all these questions as part of his job, with a supernumerary stuck in a corner listening in. He supposed the stranger in the corner was putting Mr Knight through a test.

Mr Jubb made a note.

'I gather you've been rather upset by new schemes of work in your profession, new methods,' said Mr Knight. 'Now why is that?'

'Well,' said Mr Alfred, very judicial. 'All that's said in their favour is that they're new. I don't like that. It's not a reason.'

Mr Jubb made a note.

Mr Knight turned the pages of Mr Alfred's dossier.

'You live in lodgings, I see,' he said.

'That's right,' said Mr Alfred. 'On the ground floor. It's an odd thing that. I've always had my digs on the ground floor and I've always had my classroom on the ground floor. Just as well. I hate stairs. I don't mean Sheriff Stairs.'

He smiled to encourage appreciation of his little joke. He got no smile back. Mr Knight in front of him looked past him. Mr Jubb behind him kept his head down and made a note. Mr Alfred was afraid he had said too much and said it too quickly. But he only wanted to let them see he was quite at ease.

'These new thirtytwo-storey flats,' he said slowly. I wouldn't like to live in one of them. I hate heights.'

Mr Jubb made a note.

'Why don't you take a holiday abroad?' said Mr Knight. 'You told the police you liked foreign cities, but I understand you haven't been to any of them for years. Why is that? You have a long holiday in the summer.'

'The trouble is I've got lazy,' said Mr Alfred. 'All the bother you have travelling, the customs and all that, it puts me off.'

Mr Jubb made a note.

'But if you like to be alone,' said Mr Knight, 'why do you stand in a pub every night? You're hardly alone there.'

Mr Alfred was getting rattled at the probing. He answered a bit impatiently and spoke too quickly again.

'I'm a townsman,' he said. 'I'm not keen on the wide open spaces. Mind you, I don't like to go into a pub and find nobody there. You feel too conspicuous, all that empty space at the bar. Depresses me.'

Mr Jubb made two notes.

'I like to move about where there's people,' said Mr Alfred. 'But not get mixed up with them. See what I mean?'

He moved his chair away from the radiator behind him. It was too near. He felt it scorching his bottom.

Mr Jubb made a note.

Mr Alfred saw him when he shifted his chair. He guessed there had been notes taken all the time behind his back. The suspicion that the stranger was testing him and not Mr Knight made him angry. He spoke impulsively.

'It's all these stupid buggers I've got to work with,' he said. 'They give me nightmares. You've no idea. I hate them all. All these brainless bastards and bloody bitches.'

Mr Jubb was stuck for a moment. He turned to an index page at the back of his looseleaf notebook before he made another note.

Mr Knight sighed. He stopped for coffee. As a matter of courtesy to a guest-colleague he had a word with Mr Jubb. Mr Jubb was grave.

'Do you think it's safe to let him do his own –' he paused, looked across at Mr Alfred, whispered to Mr Knight – 'pogonotomy?'

'I see no reason why he shouldn't shave himself,' said Mr Knight.

'But this fellow's not right,' said Mr Jubb. 'He's not right at all. Look at what we've found out.'

'What have we found out?' said Mr Knight.

'Children frighten him,' said Mr Knight. 'He hates fog, he's afraid to cross the street, he doesn't like strangers, he has a horror of crowds, he hates to feel people touching him, he likes to wander off on his own, he has a fear of being robbed, he was afraid of dying, he bites his nails, he wouldn't like to be senile, he drinks eight pints of beer and eight whiskies, he can't stand animals, cats give him the creeps, he loathes spiders, he doesn't like what's new, he hates climbing stairs, he hates heights, he hates travelling, he speaks too quickly, he's not keen on wide open spaces but he doesn't like empty spaces, he can't stand heat and he hates bees.'

'So?' said Mr Knight.

'Don't you see?' said Mr Jubb. 'I've got enough for another paper.'

He read off softly, softly, from his notes.

'The man's got pedophobia, homichlophobia, dromophobia, xenophobia, ochlophobia, haphephobia, planomania, kleptophobia, thanatophobia, he's an onychophagist, he's got gerontophobia, but notice he has no dysphagia, he's got zoophobia, gataphobia, arachnephobia, kainophobia, climacophobia, acrophobia, hodophobia, he suffers from intermittent tachylogia, he's got agoraphobia and kenophobia, thermophobia and melissophobia.'

'Poor soul,' said Mr Knight. 'He's in a bad way.'

'He's in a very bad way,' said Mr Jubb. 'You could have him committed for care and attention on this evidence.'

THIRTYTWO

Mr Alfred went inside for his operation while Sheriff Stairs was still considering sentence. He might have been all right, laughed at Mr Jubb, and got back to work if he hadn't taken a bad turn towards the end of his convalescence. He wakened early one morning and saw his window welcome the sun and a blue sky outside after many grey mornings. He was glad to be alive. He rose promptly and took off his pyjama-jacket. It was his habit then to put his vest on, take off his pyjama-trousers and put his pants on. This time he lifted his pants in mistake for his vest and put his arms through the legs. He knew at once there was something wrong but he wasn't sure what. He persisted in his error, trying to achieve a victory of mind over matter by simply willing the pants to become a vest. They didn't

A nurse found him reeling and writhing round his bed, his head hooded by his pants, his hands waving blindly through the brief legs. No matter how hard he butted he couldn't get his head through the crutch of his drawers. He was worried.

The nurse watched him. He gave up struggling and sat on the edge of his bed, defeated, resigned, waiting for release. He flapped his arms above his hidden head and giggled.

The nurse had met it before. She was quiet and tactful. She slipped the pants over Mr Alfred's head, drew the legs away from his arms and put him back into his pyjama-jacket and back into bed. Mr Alfred smiled and nodded. His hair was all tousled from his battle with the cul-de-sac of his drawers. He looked at the nurse with a show of intelligent interest. She tucked him in. His lips moved between his nods and smiles but he didn't really say anything.

The nurse went out. A doctor came in. Mr Alfred was sitting up, smoothing the turnover of his sheet. He gave the doctor a colleaguing smile.

When he showed more signs of deterioration he was put in a geriatric ward. He had attacks of amnesia and aphasia, but picked up a little now and again. He managed to say please without being able to say what it was he wanted. He could also say thank you when his want was understood and met. Since he wasn't all that old and beds in the geriatric ward were scarce, he was moved to a mental asylum. It may have been that crack on his skull when he was rolled in a back-close. It may have been a natural decay. He lived on without knowing. When he could speak again he was polite to everybody. He walked round the grounds twice every day, morning and afternoon, weather permitting. His only greeting to any fellow-patient he passed was a smile, a bow, and a timid murmur.

'Turned out nice again today. No sign of children.'

He would look up at the sky like a man afraid of a sudden shower.

He was suspended between heaven and earth in peace and solitude. He forgot everything else he had ever wanted. Granny Lyons came to see him three times a week, and went away crying to herself. She brought him cigarettes at first. But he didn't use them. He had forgotten about smoking. She stopped bringing them.

News always gets around. The teachers in Collinsburn heard about him and somebody raised his name once in the staffroom.

'I hadn't much use for him,' said Mr Brown. 'But I must admit I feel sorry for the poor fellow.'

'He wasn't a bad sort really,' said Mr Campbell. 'A bit pedantic sometimes maybe.'

'A bit old-fashioned,' said Mr Dale.

'Yes he was, wasn't he,' said Mr Kerr. 'Very conscientious. Never absent. Never late.'

Other people too heard about him through devious gossip.

'Haw maw!' Gerald Provan shouted one evening the moment he crossed the door. 'Know what I heard the day?'

'Naw,' said his mother standing over the frying-pan. 'What did you hear?'

'Remember big Alfy?' said Gerald.

'I'm not likely to forget him,' said Mrs Provan.

'He's been put away,' said Gerald. 'He's in the nut-house.'

'It's where he belongs,' said Mrs Provan, turning the sausages. 'Bad old bugger. He was aye mad.'

Senga at the table, waiting, listening, said nothing as Gerald gave source and details. She had left school by that time and got a job as a copy-typist in an insurance-broker's office. In spite of her squint she had a good appearance and a refined voice. She was skinny as a child, but now she was a slim, smart, confident Miss Provan. She had lost touch with Rose after the Weipers left Tordoch.

They met by chance in the street at the evening rush-hour. They had to stop and speak for old time's sake. Rose, once the prettier and more graceful, was thicklegged and broadbottomed. Her face was plump and the mouth rather slack. She was a filing-clerk in the Tax Offices in Waterloo Street.

Senga did her best but Rose had nothing much to say. They moved to the edge of the pavement to avoid obstructing people and stood staring past each other after the first awkward words. Senga was going to tell Rose about Mr Alfred, just to break the silence and make conversation. But she changed her mind at once. It might sound malicious to say he was in a mental hospital. And remembering the trouble he had caused them she thought it would be tactless to mention him at all. She tried to think of something else to say.

'I'll need to hurry,' said Rose. 'Or I won't get on a bus. I'm late.'

'Yes, I'm late too,' said Senga. 'But I'll maybe see you again sometime.'

CANONGATE CLASSICS
A NEW PERSPECTIVE FOR
SCOTTISH LITERATURE

1. Imagined Corners by Willa Muir
ISBN 0 86241 140 8

2. Consider the Lilies by Iain Crichton Smith
ISBN 0 86241 143 2

3. Island Landfalls: Reflections from the South Seas
by Robert Louis Stevenson
ISBN 0 86241 144 0

4. The Quarry Wood by Nan Shepherd
ISBN 0 86241 141 6

5. The Story of My Boyhood and Youth
by John Muir
ISBN 0 86241 153 X

6. The Land of the Leal
by James Barke
ISBN 0 86241 142 4

7. Two Worlds by David Daiches
ISBN 0 86241 148 3

8. Mr Alfred M.A.
by George Friel
ISBN 0 86241 163 7

9. The Haunted Woman
by David Lindsay
ISBN 0 86241 162 9